Lizette smiled. "I guess I could make doughnuts one of these days."

Judd told himself that it was only his concern for the safety of the kids that made him worry about who was likely to be visiting the ballet school. He'd been in Dry Creek long enough to know about all the cowboys on the outlying ranches.

A woman like Lizette Baker was bound to attract enough attention without adding doughnuts to the equation.

Not that it should matter to him how many men gawked at the ballet teacher. He certainly wasn't going to cause any awkwardness by being overly friendly himself. He was just hoping to get to know her a little better.

She was, after all, the kids' teacher, and he was, for the time being, their parent. It was practically his civic duty to be friendly to her. And he didn't need a doughnut to make him realize it.

Books by Janet Tronstad

Love Inspired

*An Angel for Dry Creek #81
*A Gentleman for Dry Creek #110
*A Bride for Dry Creek #138
*A Rich Man for Dry Creek #176
*A Hero for Dry Creek #228
*A Baby for Dry Creek #240
*A Dry Creek Christmas #276
*Sugar Plums for Dry Creek #329

*Dry Creek

JANET TRONSTAD

grew up on a small farm in central Montana. One of her favorite things to do was to visit her grandfather's bookshelves, where he had a large collection of Zane Grey novels. She's always loved a good story.

Today, Janet lives in Pasadena, California. In addition to writing novels, she researches and writes nonfiction magazine articles.

SUGAR PLUMS
FOR DRY CREEK
JANET TRONSTAD

Steeple
Hill®

Published by Steeple Hill Books™

STEEPLE HILL BOOKS

Steeple
Hill®

ISBN 0-373-87339-5

SUGAR PLUMS FOR DRY CREEK

Copyright © 2005 by Janet Tronstad

www.SteepleHill.com

Printed in U.S.A.

I can do all things through Christ
which strengtheneth me.
—*Philippians* 4:13

This book is dedicated to my grandfather,
Harold Norris, who shared his love of
a good book with me.

Chapter One

Lizette Baker wished her mother had worried less about showing her the perfect way to pirouette and more about teaching her a few practical things, like how to coax more warm air out of her old car's heating system and how to put snow chains on tires so smooth they slipped on every icy patch she found as she drove east on Interstate 94 in southern Montana.

A colder, frostier place Lizette had never seen. Even with a wool scarf wrapped around her neck and mittens on her hands, she couldn't stay warm. It was only mid-November and it was already less than ten degrees Fahrenheit outside. No wonder hers was the only car in sight as she drove along this road hoping to reach Dry Creek, Montana, before her heater gave out completely.

The attendant in the gas station she'd stopped at back in Forsyth had offered to call a mechanic to repair her heater. Another man, with a dirty blond beard and a snake tattooed on his arm, had made a different suggestion.

"Why put out good money for a mechanic?" he'd asked in an artificially friendly voice. Lizette hadn't liked the way he was looking at her. "I'll keep you warm if you give me a ride down the road a bit. I'm looking for my kids." He'd reached into his pocket and pulled out a worn snapshot, which he'd then shoved at her. "Kids need to see their old man. You haven't seen them, have you?"

Lizette would have rather given the snake on the man's arm a ride than the man himself, but she hadn't wanted any trouble, so she'd politely looked at the picture of his two children.

"No, but they're beautiful children." And the children probably would have been beautiful, she thought, if they hadn't looked so skinny and scared. "Sorry about the ride, but I have a car full of boxes. Moving, you know."

Lizette hoped the man hadn't looked at her car too closely. If she'd shifted the boxes around a little, she could have cleared enough room in the front seat for a passenger.

The tattooed man hadn't said anything more, but he'd put the picture back in his pocket.

After a moment's silence, the attendant had finally

asked, "So do you want the mechanic to come over to fix that heater? He doesn't keep regular hours, but he can get down here in fifteen minutes flat."

Lizette had shaken her head. "Thanks though."

She barely had enough money left to get her ballet school going; she couldn't afford to fix anything that wasn't actually falling off the car. The heater was spitting out just enough warm air to keep her from freezing to death, so it would have to do for now.

She'd looked out her rearview mirror as she'd pulled away from the gas station and had seen the man with the snake on his arm watching her leave.

It wasn't the first time since she'd left Seattle that Lizette had wondered if she was making a mistake.

Her whole life had changed in the last few months though, and she needed a new beginning. Besides, where else could she get free rent to start her own business? Lizette had learned to be frugal from her mother, Jacqueline. Indeed, it had been Jacqueline who'd found the ad for free space.

Lizette had not known until recently that her mother had saved for years with the hope that they could open their own ballet school someday. When Lizette's father had died, years ago, Jacqueline had given up the fledgling ballet school she and her husband had started and had taken a steady job in a bakery. At the time, Lizette had not realized the sacrifice her mother was making to keep them secure, probably because Jacqueline never complained about giving up the school. When she'd first tied on her bakery apron, she'd even managed to joke. She said she wished her husband could see her. He'd say she was really a Baker at last.

Her mother had made the job sound as though it was exactly what she wanted, and Lizette had believed her back then. Maybe that was because Lizette herself was happy. The bakery was a playground to her. She loved the warm smells and all of the chatter of customers. The bakers even got into the habit of asking Lizette to try out their new recipes. They said she had a taste for what the customers would like.

Giving up that ballet school was only one of the many sacrifices Jacqueline Baker had made for Lizette over the years. Lizette hadn't even known about some of them until her mother had been diagnosed with terminal cancer. That's when she'd started giving instructions to Lizette.

"You'll find fifteen thousand dollars in this safety deposit box," Jacqueline told her as she handed Lizette a key. "I wanted it to be more, but it'll get that school of ours started if we're careful. Then there'll be no need for you to work at the bakery—you'll be free to dance. The money should cover everything for a year. We don't need anything expensive—just something with good floors and lots of room for practice."

Lizette was amazed and touched. So that was why her mother'd never spent much money on herself, not even after she became the manager of the bakery and started earning a better salary. Lizette could see how important it was to her mother to start what she was calling the Baker School of Ballet.

As the pain increased and Jacqueline went into the hospital, she talked more and more about the school. She worried that Lizette had not been able to find an affordable space to rent even though she'd gone out to look at several places. Jacqueline even asked the hospital chaplain to come and pray about it.

Lizette was surprised her mother was interested in praying. Jacqueline had shown little use for God over the years, saying she could not understand a God who took a man away in his prime. Unspoken was the complaint that He had also robbed her of her beloved ballet school at the same time.

But now, at the end, who did her mother want to talk to? The chaplain.

If they hadn't been in a hospital when her mother asked to speak to a minister, Lizette wouldn't even have known how to find one. She herself had never been to church in her life. Sunday was the one day she could spend with her mother, and Jacqueline made it clear she didn't want to go to church, so Lizette never even suggested it.

Yet on her deathbed Lizette's mother spent hours talking to the chaplain about her hopes for a ballet school. Lizette quietly apologized to the man one afternoon when the two of them had left the room so the nurse could give Jacqueline an injection. Lizette knew the chaplain was a busy man, and she doubted he was interested in ballet schools—especially ones that didn't even exist except in a dying woman's dreams.

The chaplain waved Lizette's apology aside, "Your mother's talking about her life when she talks about that school. That's what I'm here for. It's important."

In the last days, the soft sound of the chaplain's praying was all that quieted Jacqueline. Well, Lizette acknowledged, toward the end it was also those expensive injections that kept her mother comfortable. Lizette never did tell Jacqueline that those injections weren't covered by their insurance plan.

It didn't take much money to open a ballet school, Lizette told herself when her mother kept asking about sites. By then, the extra hospital bills had used up the entire fifteen thousand dollars, and Lizette's small savings account as well. Lizette said a prayer of her own when she promised to open the school in the fall.

"You're right. Fall is the best time of the year to start a ballet school," Jacqueline said as she lay in her hospital bed. "We can start our students right out on our simplified version of the Nutcracker ballet, and they'll be hooked. Every young girl wants to be Clara. Plus we already have all of those costumes we made for you and the other girls when you were in dance school."

Part of the deal in the sale of her parents' ballet school had been that the new owner, Madame Aprele, would give Lizette free lessons. Lizette had studied ballet for years, and even though she didn't have her mother's natural grace, she still did very well.

"And you'll be there to watch." Lizette dreamed a little dream of her own. "You've always loved the Nutcracker."

Her mother smiled. "I can almost see it now. I remember the first time I danced Clara as a five-year-old. And later, the Sugar Plum Fairy. What I wouldn't give to dance it all again!"

Lizette vowed she'd find a way to open a school even without money. Then maybe her mother would get stronger and they could run that school together. With all of the praying the chaplain was doing, Lizette figured they were due a miracle.

Later that week Jacqueline claimed she'd found a miracle—right in the middle of the classified section of *The Seattle Times*. The ad offering free rent for new businesses had been buried in the used furniture section of the paper. Lizette called the phone number from the hospital room so her mother could listen to her end of the conversation.

Free rent would solve all of their problems for the school, and Lizette wanted Jacqueline to share the excitement of the phone call. Lizette hadn't realized until she was halfway through the conversation that the free rent was in a small town in Montana.

Jacqueline kept nodding at her during the conversation, so Lizette found herself agreeing to take the town of Dry Creek up on their offer. She couldn't disappoint her mother by telling her that the free rent wasn't in Seattle.

Of course, Lizette had no intention of actually going to Dry Creek, Montana. She knew nothing about the place. Something about the phone call calmed Jacqueline, however, and she seemed truly satisfied. The chaplain said she made her peace with God the next afternoon. After that, nothing Lizette did could stop her mother from slipping away.

After Jacqueline was gone, Lizette remembered the small town in Montana. Seattle seemed the emptiest city in the world without her mother. Lizette couldn't stay at the bakery, even though she'd worked there for the past six years. Lizette enjoyed the job, but she knew her mother would have scolded her for hiding away there.

Besides baking, the only other skill Lizette had was her expertise in ballet and there were no jobs for young ballet teachers in Seattle. Oh, Madame Aprele offered her a job, but Lizette knew the small school didn't need another teacher, and she wasn't desperate enough to take charity.

No, she had to go somewhere else, and she didn't much care where.

So, here she was—moving to Dry Creek, Montana, and all because of a phone conversation with an old man and an offer of free rent. Lizette wasn't sure the school would work. A small town in eastern Montana wasn't the place she would have chosen to open the Baker School of Ballet.

Not that it was absolutely the worst place to start, Lizette assured herself. So few people appreciated ballet these days, and it gladdened her heart to remember the enthusiasm in the old man's voice when she had called in response to the ad. The man she'd talked to on the phone was gruff, and she couldn't always hear him because of the static, but he seemed excited that she was taking the town up on their offer of six months' free rent. He kept talking about how large the area was that they could set aside for her.

The old man had mentioned tables and chairs and counters, so he might not be too familiar with ballet, but Lizette wouldn't let that discourage her. It was the enthusiasm in his heart that counted. She'd be happy to educate this little town on the finer points of ballet.

Lizette was going to go ahead with a modified Nutcracker ballet. Her mother had been right that it was a great way to start. Lizette decided she would even make Sugar Plum pastries for a little reception after the performance. Stuffed with dried plums and vanilla custard, they were a Christmas favorite with many of the customers at the bakery.

The people of Dry Creek would like them as well.

Yes, Lizette thought to herself. A little music, a little ballet and a cream-filled pastry—the people of Dry Creek would be glad she'd opened her school in their town.

Chapter Two

Judd Bowman was standing at the back of the hardware store in Dry Creek counting nails. He figured he needed about fifty nails, but every time he got to thirty or so, one of the kids would interrupt him because they had to go to the bathroom or they wanted a drink of water or they thought they heard a kitten meowing. Judd sighed. Trying to take care of a six-year-old boy and a five-year-old girl was no picnic. Fortunately, the hardware store had a heater going, and it took the edge off the cold.

"Just sit down until I finish," Judd said when he felt Amanda's arm brush against his leg. He'd gotten to thirty-seven, and he repeated the number to himself. He knew the kids needed reassurance, so he tried to speak two sentences when one would have done him fine. "I won't be long and then we can go over to the café and have some cocoa. You like cocoa, don't you?"

Judd felt Amanda nod against his knee. He looked over to see that Bobby was still drawing a picture on the piece of paper that the man who ran the hardware store had given him earlier.

Amanda seemed to squeeze even closer to his knee, and Judd looked down. She was pale and clutching his pant leg in earnest now as she stared around his leg at the men in the middle of the hardware store.

Judd looked over at them, wondering what had stirred up the old men who sat around the potbellied stove. Usually, when he came into the store, the men were dozing quietly in their chairs around the fire or playing a slow game of chess.

Today, with the cold seeping into the store, the fire was almost out. There was wood in the basket nearby, so there was no excuse for anyone not to put another log in the stove.

But the men weren't paying any attention to the cold or the fire.

Instead, they were all looking out the window of the hardware store and across the street into the window of what had been an old abandoned store that stood next to the café. The store wasn't abandoned any longer. Judd could see the woman as she tried to hang what looked like a sign on the inside of her window.

Judd didn't usually pay much attention to women, but he'd have remembered this one if he'd seen her before. She was tall and graceful, with her black hair twisted into a knot on the top of head. He could see why men would be looking at her.

"They're just talking," Judd said as he rested his hand on Amanda's shoulder.

Judd had little use for idle conversation, but even he had heard a week ago that a new woman was moving to town. Several months ago the town had placed an ad in *The Seattle Times* inviting businesses to move to Dry Creek. The town had sweetened the deal by offering six months of free rent. Even at that, the woman was the only one to actually agree to come, so the town had given her the best of the old buildings they owned.

Judd squeezed Amanda's shoulder as Bobby walked over to stand beside them as well. The boy had become attuned to his sister's moods, and it never took him long to know when Amanda was frightened.

Judd spoke softly. "They're just talking about the new woman who moved here."

"Remember I told you about her?" Bobby added as he leaned down to look his sister in the eye. "She's going to make doughnuts."

"I'm not sure about the doughnuts," Judd said. He worked hard to keep his voice even. Amanda picked up too easily on the emotion in men's voices, and even though Judd was angry at the man who had made her so sensitive and not at *her,* he knew she'd think he was upset with her if he let his voice be anything but neutral.

Getting involved in the problems of Dry Creek was the last thing Judd wanted to do, but if that's what it took to help Amanda realize all anger wasn't directed at her, then that's what he'd have to do. "Let's go see what it's all about."

Judd walked slowly enough so Amanda could keep her fingers wrapped around his leg. She had her other hand in Bobby's small hand.

"How's it going?" Judd asked when they arrived at the group around the stove.

Judd had seen these men a dozen times since he'd rented the Jenkins farm this past spring, but he'd been so busy all summer with farm work and then with the kids that this was the first time he'd done more than nod in their direction.

Fortunately, the men were all too steamed up to wonder why he chose to talk now.

"Charley here is going deaf," Jacob muttered as he leaned back with his fingers in his suspenders.

"I am not," Charley said as he looked up at Judd through his bifocals. "I had a bad connection on that new fangled cell phone. Don't know what's wrong with it. Some of the words don't come through too clear."

"That's when you ask the person to repeat themselves," Jacob said.

The two men had obviously had this conversation before.

"I was being friendly," Charley protested as he stood up and looked straight at Judd. "Everyone kept telling me to be friendly if anyone called. Now, do you think it sounds friendly to keep asking someone to repeat what they've just said?"

"Well, I guess that depends." Judd hesitated. He didn't want to get involved in the argument. He just wanted Amanda to hear that it wasn't about her.

"You know, I got that phone because everybody said people would be calling about the ad at all times of the night and day," Charley complained as he sat back down. "I even carried it to bed with me. And this is the thanks I get."

"So you're all angry because of the phone." Judd nodded. There. That should satisfy Amanda that the argument had nothing to do with her.

"It isn't the phone," Jacob said as he shook his head. "It's what he was supposed to do with the phone. He was supposed to make sure that businesses were suitable for Dry Creek."

"He said she was a baker!" another old man protested.

"I had my mouth all set for a doughnut," Jacob admitted. "One of those long maple ones."

"Well, she kept saying Baker," Charley defended

himself. "How was I supposed to know that was just her name? Dry Creek could use a good bakery."

"But she's not a baker. She runs a dance school!" Jacob protested.

"And that's the problem?" Judd tried again. He could feel Amanda's hold on his leg lessen. She was listening to the men.

"Of course that's the problem," Jacob continued. "She doesn't even teach *real* dancing, like the stomp-and-holler stuff they have at the senior center up by Miles City. This here is ballet. Who around here wants to learn ballet? You have to wear tights."

"Or a tutu," another old man added. "Pink fluffy stuff."

"It isn't decent, if you ask me," still another man muttered. "Don't know where she'll buy all that netting around here anyway."

"The store here started carrying bug netting since the mosquitoes were so bad over the summer. They still have some left. Maybe she could use that," the first old man offered.

"She can't use bug netting," Charley said. "Not for ballet. Besides, she probably wants it to be pink, and that bug netting is black."

"Well, of course it's black," another old man said. "Mosquitoes don't care if it's some fancy color."

"Netting is the least of her worries. She isn't going

to have any students, so she won't need any netting," Jacob finally said.

There was a moment's silence.

"Maybe she *will* take up baking—to keep herself busy if she doesn't have any students," Charley offered. "I heard she was trying to make some kind of cookies."

"They burnt," another man said mournfully. "The smoke came clear over here. I went over and asked if maybe a pie would be easier to bake."

"She's not going to be making pies. She's going to go around trying to change the people of Dry Creek into something we're not. It's like trying to turn a pig into a silk purse. I say just let a pig be a pig—the way God intended," Jacob said.

Judd looked down at Amanda. She'd stopped holding on to his pants leg and was listening intently to the men. He was glad she was listening even if she wasn't talking yet. In the three months that Judd had been taking care of the two kids, Amanda occasionally whispered something to her brother, but she never said anything to anyone else, not even Judd.

Amanda leaned over to whisper in Bobby's ear now.

The boy smiled and nodded. "Yeah, she *is* awfully pretty."

Bobby looked up at the men. "Amanda thinks the woman looks like our mama."

Judd's breath caught. Both kids had stopped talking

about their mother a month ago. Barbara was his second cousin, but Judd hadn't known her until she showed up on his doorstep one morning. She'd paid an agency to find him because she wanted to ask him to take care of her kids while she got settled in a place. She was on the run from an abusive husband and had the court papers to prove it.

Judd had refused Barbara's request at first. Sheer disbelief had cleared his mind of anything else. Judd had never known his mother, and the uncle who had raised him had been more interested in having a hired hand that he didn't need to pay than in parenting an orphan. The stray dog Judd had taken in earlier in the summer probably knew more about family life than Judd did. Judd wasn't someone anyone had ever thought to leave kids with before this. And one look at the kids showed him that they were still in the napping years.

"You must have taken care of little ones before—" Barbara had said.

"Not unless they had four feet and a tail," Judd told her firmly. He'd nursed calves and stray dogs and even a pony or two. But kids? Never.

No, Judd wasn't the one his cousin needed. "You'll need to find someone else. Believe me, it's best."

"But—" Barbara said and then swallowed.

Judd didn't like the look of desperation he saw in her eyes.

"You're our only family," she finally finished.

Judd figured she probably had that about right. The Bowman family tree had always been more of a stump than anything. Ever since his uncle had died, Judd had thought he was the last of the line.

Still, he hesitated.

He thought of suggesting she turn to the state for help, but he knew what kind of trouble that could get her into. Once children were in the state system, it wasn't all that easy to get them out again, and he could see by the way she kept looking at the kids that she loved them.

He might not know much about a mother's love himself, but he could at least recognize it when he saw it.

"Maybe you could get a babysitter," Judd finally offered. "Some nice grandmother or something."

"You know someone like that?"

Judd had to admit he didn't. He'd only moved to Dry Creek this past spring. He'd been working long and hard plowing and then seeding the alfalfa and wheat crops. He hadn't taken time to get to know any of his neighbors yet.

He wished now that he had accepted one of the invitations to church he'd received since he'd been here. An older woman, Mrs. Hargrove, had even driven out to the ranch one day and invited him. She'd looked so friendly he'd almost promised to go, but he didn't.

What would a man like him do in church anyway?

He wouldn't know when to kneel or when to sing or when to bow his head. No, church wasn't for him.

Now he wished he had gone to church anyway, even if he'd made a fool of himself doing so. Mrs. Hargrove would probably help someone who went to her church. She wasn't likely to help a stranger though. Who would be?

"Maybe we could put an ad in the paper."

Barbara just looked at him. "We don't have time for that."

Judd had to admit she was right.

"Besides, this is something big—the kind of thing family members do to help each other," Barbara said with such conviction that Judd believed her.

Not that he was an expert on what family members did to help each other. He couldn't remember his uncle ever doing him a kindness, and the man was the only family Judd had ever known. His uncle had lost all contact with his cousin who was Barbara's father.

He had to admit he had been excited at first when Barbara had come to his doorstep. It was nice to think he had family somewhere in this world.

He looked over at the kids and saw that they were sitting still as stones. Kids shouldn't be so quiet.

"Are they trained?" he asked.

Barbara looked at him blankly for a moment. "You mean potty-trained?"

He nodded.

"Of course! Amanda here is five years old. And Bobby is six. They practically take care of themselves."

Barbara didn't pause before she continued. "And it might only be for a few days. Just enough time for me to drive down to Denver and check out that women's shelter. I want to be sure they'll take us before I drag the kids all that way."

Barbara had arrived in an old car that had seen better days, but it had gotten her here, so Judd figured it would get her to Denver.

Still, if she had car trouble, he knew it would be hard to take care of the kids while she saw to getting the thing fixed. He supposed—maybe—

"I guess things will be slow for the next few days," Judd said. He'd finished putting up the hay, and he had enough of the fence built so his thirty head of cattle could graze in the pasture by the creek. He meant to spend the next few days working on the inside of the house anyway before he turned back to building the rest of the fence. He supposed two trained kids wouldn't be too much trouble.

Judd didn't exactly say he'd keep the kids, but he guessed Barbara could tell he'd lowered his resistance, because she turned her attention to the kids, telling them they were going to stay with Cousin Judd and she'd be back in a few days. That was at the end of August. It was mid-November now.

Judd still hadn't finished all of the fencing, and it was already starting to snow some. If he waited any longer, the ground would be frozen too far down to dig fence holes. That's why he was at the hardware store today getting nails and talking to the old men by the stove.

Judd watched the old men as they smiled at the kids now.

Jacob nodded slowly as he looked at Amanda. "I saw your mama when she brought you and your brother here. She stopped to ask directions. You're right, she was pretty, too."

"My mama's going to come back and get us real soon," Bobby said.

Jacob nodded. "I expect she will."

Judd gave him a curt nod of thanks. Barbara had asked for a few days, but Judd had figured he'd give her a week. By now, she was at least two months overdue to pick up the kids.

Judd hadn't told the kids he'd contacted the court that had issued the restraining order their mother had flashed in front of him and asked them to help find her. Fortunately Barbara had listed him as her next of kin on some paper they had. The court clerk had called every women's shelter between here and Denver and hadn't located Judd's cousin.

Judd had had to do some persuasive talking to the

clerk, because he didn't want to mention the kids. He figured his cousin needed a chance to come back for them on her own.

"She's just hurt her hand so she can't write and tell us when," Bobby added confidently.

"I expect that's right. Mail sometimes takes a while," Jacob agreed, and then added, "but then it only makes the letter more special when you do get it."

The older men shifted in their seats. Judd knew they were all aware of the troubles Amanda and Bobby were having. They might not know the details, but he had told his landlady, Linda, back in the beginning of September that he was watching the children for his cousin for a couple of weeks. By now, everyone in Dry Creek probably knew there was something wrong.

Even if he was a newcomer, he would be foolish to think they hadn't asked each other why the kids were still here. Of course, the old men were polite and wouldn't ask a direct question, at least not in front of the kids, so they probably didn't know how bad it all was. They probably thought Barbara had called and made arrangements for the kids to stay longer.

"Speaking of letters, maybe we could write a letter to the new woman and tell her we all want a bakery more than a ballet school," Charley finally broke the silence with a suggestion.

"We can't do that," Jacob said with a sigh. "You don't write a letter to someone who's right across the street. No, we need to be neighborly and tell her to her face. It isn't fair that we let her think she'll make a go of it here with that school of hers."

"Well, I can't talk to her," Charley said. "I'm the one who promised her everything would be fine."

"Too bad *she* wasn't the one who was deaf," one of the other men muttered.

"I'm not deaf. I had a bad connection is all," Charley said. "It could happen to anyone."

"Maybe *he* could go talk to her," the other man said, looking up at Judd. "He seems to hear all right."

Judd felt his stomach knot up at the idea. "I got to count me out some nails. I'm building a fence."

He walked back to the shelves that held the boxes of nails. Amanda and Bobby trailed along after him. Judd looked down at Bobby. "Why don't you take your sister and go across to the café and put your order in for some of that cocoa? Tell Linda I'll be along in a minute."

The Linda who ran the café was also his landlady. She was renting him the Jenkins place, with an option to buy come next spring. Judd had saved the few thousand dollars the state had given him when it settled his uncle's estate and added most of the other money he'd gotten to it for the past six years.

He'd started out working as a ranch hand, but the wages added up too slowly for him, and so he'd spent the next couple of years on the rodeo circuit. He'd earned enough in prize money to set himself up nicely. Right now, he had enough money in the bank to buy the Jenkins place, and he'd already stocked it with some purebred breeding cattle. He could have bought the place outright, but he wanted to take his time and be sure he liked it well enough before he made the final deal. So far, the ground had been fertile and the place quiet enough to suit him.

Judd watched Amanda and Bobby leave the hardware store before he reached into the nail bin and pulled out another nail. Fortunately, the older men had given up on the idea that he should talk to the new woman. They probably realized he'd botch the job.

Outside of talking with Linda at the café and smiling politely when Mrs. Hargrove had delivered the books the school had sent him when he'd decided to homeschool the kids, Judd hadn't had a conversation with a woman since his cousin had left the kids with him. Well, unless you counted the court clerk he'd talked to on the phone.

Judd never had been much good at talking to women, at least not women who weren't rodeo followers. He had no problem with women at rodeos, probably because *they* did most of the talking and he always knew what they wanted; they wanted a rodeo winner to escort them around town for the evening. That didn't exactly require conversation, not with the yelling that spilled out of most rodeo hangouts in the evening.

As long as his boots were polished and his hat on straight, the rodeo women didn't care if he was quiet. He was mostly for show anyway—if he was winning. If he wasn't winning, they weren't that interested in talking to him, or even interested in being with him.

The few temporary affairs he'd had with rodeo followers didn't leave him feeling good about himself, so eventually he just declined invitations to party. By then he was counting up his prize money after every rodeo anyway, with an eye to when he could leave the circuit and set himself up on his own ranch.

In those years, Judd hadn't known any women outside of rodeo circles, and he thought that was best. Judd never seemed to know what those women were thinking, and he didn't even try to sort it all out. He liked things straightforward and to the point. The other kind of women—the kind that made wives—always seemed to say things in circles and then expect a man to know what they meant. For all Judd knew, they could be speaking Greek.

Judd had a feeling the new woman in Dry Creek was one of that kind of women.

No, he wasn't the one to talk to her about what she was doing here, even though he had to admit he was curious. She sure knew how to hang a sign in that window.

Chapter Three

Lizette shifted the sign with her left hand and took a deep breath. It had taken her the better part of three days to get the practice bar in place along the left side of the room and the floor waxed to a smooth shine. She still had the costumes hanging on a rack near the door waiting to be sorted by size, but she'd decided this morning it was time to put the sign she'd made in her window and start advertising for students.

She could still smell the floor wax, so she'd opened the door to air out the room even though it was cold outside. At least it wasn't snowing today.

Lizette had bought a large piece of metal at the hardware store yesterday and some paint so she could make her sign. The old men sitting around the stove in the store had obviously heard she was setting up a business, because they were full of suggestions on how she should make her sign.

Of course, most of the words centered on the Baker part of the school's name, but she couldn't fault them for that. She was heartened to see they had so much enthusiasm for a ballet school. If this was any indication of the interest of the rest of the people in the community, she just might get enough students to pull off a modified Nutcracker ballet for Christmas after all. She'd even assured the men in the hardware store that no one was too old to learn some ballet steps. In fact, she'd told them that lots of athletes used ballet as a way to exercise.

The old men had looked a little dismayed at her comments, and she wasn't surprised. At their age, they probably didn't want to take up *any* exercise program, especially not one as rigorous as ballet. "You'd want to check with your doctor first, of course," Lizette added. "You should do that before you take up any new exercise program."

The men nodded as she left the hardware store. All in all, they'd been friendly, and she wasn't so sure she wouldn't get a student or two out of the bunch. And if she didn't get any students, at least she'd gotten some good neighbors. One of them had already been over to check on the smoke coming out of the small kitchen off the main room when she'd been baking some cookies earlier and had forgotten they were in the oven. He'd even offered to bring her over some more flour if she was inclined to continue baking. He'd expressed some hope of a cherry pie.

The chair Lizette stood on gave her enough height so she could lift the sign and hook it into the chain she'd put up to hang it with. The sign had a white background with navy script lettering.

Lizette planned to take a picture of the sign later and send it to Madame Aprele. She wasn't sure she'd tell her old teacher that she didn't have any students yet, but she could tell her that the school was almost ready for classes now that the practice bar was in place. Lizette had planned to use a makeshift practice bar at first, because she couldn't afford a real one. Madame Aprele had surprised her by sending her one of her own mahogany bars. Her old teacher had shipped it before Lizette left Seattle, and Linda, next door in the café, had kept it for Lizette until she arrived.

Lizette had called Madame Aprele, thanking her and insisting that she accept payment for the equipment. It would help enough, Lizette explained, if she could just pay for the bar over time. She didn't add that she had no need of charity. Madame Aprele agreed to let Lizette make payments if Lizette promised to call her with weekly updates on her school.

At first Lizette was uncomfortable promising to call Madame Aprele, because she knew her mother would disapprove. But then Lizette decided that whatever problem there had been between her mother and Madame Aprele, there was no need for *her* to continue the coldness.

Twenty years ago when Madame Aprele had bought the school from Lizette's mother, the two women had been friends. But, over the years, Jacqueline spoke less and less to Madame Aprele until, finally, her mother wouldn't even greet the other women when she picked Lizette up after ballet class.

At the time, Lizette didn't understand why. Now she wondered if her mother didn't look at Madame Aprele and wish her own life had turned out like the other woman's.

Not that there was anything in Jacqueline's life to suggest she wished for a different one. Madame Aprele had been born in France in the same village as Lizette's mother. Both women had studied ballet together and had left France together. Lizette's mother had become more Americanized over the years, however, especially after she'd started working in the bakery.

As Lizette's mother became more conservative in her dress, Madame Aprele became more outrageous, until, in the end, Lizette's mother looked almost dowdy and Madame Aprele looked like an old-fashioned movie star with her lavender feather boas and dramatic eye makeup.

* * *

Lizette stepped down from the chair just as she saw two little children cross the street from the hardware store. The sun was shining on the window so Lizette could not see the children clearly, but she could tell from their size that they were both good prospects for ballet.

Lizette didn't know how to advertise in a small town like Dry Creek, but she supposed she could ask about the children at the hardware store, find out who their parents were and send them a flyer.

When the children passed her door, they stopped. The little girl was staring at something, and it didn't take long for Lizette to figure out what it was. The sunlight was streaming in, making the Sugar Plum Fairy costume sparkle even more than usual. Lizette's mother had used both gold and metallic pink on the costume when she'd made it, and many a young girl mistook it for a princess costume.

"If you go ask your mother if it's okay, you can come in and look at the costumes," Lizette said. She doubted things were so casual in Dry Creek that parents wanted their children going into strange stores without their knowledge.

The girl whispered something in the boy's ear. He nodded.

Lizette had walked closer to the children and was

starting to feel uneasy. If you added a few pounds and took away the scared look in their eyes, those two kids looked very similar to that snapshot she'd seen several days ago. She looked up and down the snow-covered street. There were the usual cars and pickups parked beside the hardware store and the café, but there were no people outside except for the two children. "Does your mother know where you are?"

Both children solemnly nodded their heads yes.

Lizette was relieved to know the children had a mother. Their father hadn't looked like much of a parent, but hopefully their mother was better.

"Our mother won't mind if we look at the dress," the boy politely said after a moment and pointed inside. "That one."

The rack was very close to the door and Lizette decided she could leave the door open so the children's mother could see them if she looked down the street. Really, if she moved the rack closer, the children could touch the costumes while they stood outside on the sidewalk.

Lizette pushed the costume rack so it was just inside the door. "The pink one is my favorite, too."

Lizette watched as the little girl reached out her hand and gently touched the costume.

"That's the dress for the Sugar Plum Fairy in the Nutcracker ballet," Lizette said.

"What's a ballet?" the boy asked.

Lizette thought a moment. "It's like a play with lots of costumes and people moving."

"So someone wears that dress in a play?" the boy asked.

The boy and Lizette were both seeing the same thing. The little girl's face was starting to glow. One moment she had been pale and quiet, and the next her face started to show traces of pink and her eyes started to sparkle.

For the first time, Lizette decided she had made the right decision to come to Dry Creek to open her school. If there were more little girls and boys like this in the community, she'd have a wonderful time teaching them to love ballet.

Chapter Four

Lizette heard a sound and looked up to see a half-dozen men stomping down the steps of the hardware store and heading straight toward her new school. She wasn't sure, but she thought every one of the men was frowning, especially the one who was at the back of the group. That man had to be forty years younger than the other men, but he looked the most annoyed of them all.

"The children are still just on the sidewalk," Lizette said when the men were close enough to hear. While she hadn't thought anyone would want children to go into a building alone, she certainly hadn't expected there would be a problem with them standing on the sidewalk and looking at something inside. If the citizens of Dry Creek were that protective of their children, she'd never have any young students in her classes.

Lizette braced herself, but when the men reached

her, they stood silent. Finally, one of them cleared his throat, "About this—ah—school—"

"The children will all have permission from their parents, of course," Lizette rushed to assure them. "And parents can watch the classes any time they want. They can even attend if they want. I'd love to have some older students."

The younger man, the one who had hung back on the walk over, moved closer to the open door. He seemed intent on the two children and did not stop until he stood beside them protectively. Lizette noticed that the young boy relaxed a little when the man stood beside him, and the girl reached out her hand to touch the man's leg. She knew the man wasn't the children's father because she'd met that man already. Maybe he was their stepfather. That would explain why the father hadn't known where the children lived.

"Well, about the students—" The older man cleared his throat and began again. "You see, there might be a problem with students."

"No one has to audition or anything to be in the performances," Lizette said. She wasn't sure what was bothering the men, but she wanted them to know she was willing to work with the town. "And public performance is good for children, especially if it's not competitive."

"Anyone can be in the play," the boy said softly.

The men had all stopped talking to listen to the boy, so they all heard the next words very clearly.

"I'm going to be a Sugar Plum Fairy," the girl said, and pointed to the costume she'd been admiring.

Judd swallowed. Amanda never talked to anyone but Bobby, and then only in whispers. Who knew all it would take was a sparkly costume to make her want to talk?

"How much is the costume?" Judd asked the woman in the doorway. He didn't care what figure she named— he'd buy it for Amanda.

"Oh, the costumes aren't for sale," the woman said. "I'll need them for the performance, especially if I want to have something ready for Christmas. I won't have time to make many more costumes."

"About this performance—" The older man said, then cleared his throat.

Lizette wondered what was bothering the old man, but she didn't have time to ask him because the younger man was scowling at her.

"So the only way Amanda can wear this costume is if she's in your performance?" he asked.

"I wouldn't say it was *my* performance." Lizette felt her patience starting to grow thin. "All of the students will see it as *their* performance. We work together."

"About the students—" The older man began again and cleared his throat for what must have been the fourth time.

"I'll sign Amanda up," the younger man said decisively. "If she signs up first, she should get her pick of the parts, shouldn't she?"

"Well, I don't see why she can't be the Sugar Plum Fairy," Lizette agreed. After all, Lizette herself would be choreographing the part for the children's ballet, and could tailor it to Amanda's skills. She'd just gotten her first student. "She'll have to practice, of course. And we'll have to have a few more students to do even a shortened version of the Nutcracker."

The younger man squeezed the boy on his shoulder.

"I'll sign up, too," the boy offered reluctantly.

"There—I have two students!" Lizette announced triumphantly. "And I only just hung up my sign."

The older man cleared his throat again, but this time he had nothing to say. All of the older men were looking a little stunned. Maybe they were as taken aback as she was by the fierce scowl the younger man was giving them.

"You might want to see a doctor about the cold you're getting," Lizette finally said to the man who had been trying to talk. "Usually when you have to clear your throat so often, it means a cold is coming on."

The older man nodded silently.

"And you might ask him about taking up ballet while you're there," Lizette said. "Just to see if the exercise would be all right for you. Now that I have two students, I can begin classes, and you'd be more than welcome."

Lizette decided the older man definitely had a cold coming on. He had just gone pale. He even looked a little dizzy.

"You'll want to wait until you're feeling better before you start though," Lizette said to him. That seemed to make him feel better. At least his color returned.

"I'll think about it," he mumbled.

Lizette nodded. She knew she couldn't manage for long on the income she'd get from two students, but just look how much people wanted to talk about her school. With all of that talk, she'd get more students before long.

Lizette smiled up at the younger man. He might scowl a lot, but she was grateful to him for her first two students. "Your wife must be happy you take such good care of the children."

The young man looked down at her. "I don't have a wife."

Lizette faltered. "Oh, I just thought that because their father showed me their picture that—"

"You know the kids' father, Neal Strong?"

If Lizette thought the men had been quiet before, they were even more silent now.

"No, I don't know him. Some man just showed me their picture in Forsyth when he asked me to give him a ride out this way. He said they were his kids and he was trying to find them. He probably didn't know the address or something."

Judd felt Amanda move closer to his leg, and suddenly he had as great a need to be close to her as she had to be close to him, so he reached down and lifted her up even though he had his heavy farm coat on and it probably had grease on it from when he'd last worked on the tractor.

"Don't worry," Judd whispered into Amanda's hair when she snuggled into his shoulder.

Judd reminded himself that the papers Barbara had shown him when she left the children with him included a court order forbidding the children's father from being within one hundred yards of them.

Judd knew the court clerk well enough now that he could ask for a copy of the court order if he needed one. Of course, that would mean the clerk would guess that the children were with him. No, there had to be another way. Besides, he didn't actually need a copy of the order for the court to enforce it.

"You're sure it was him?" Judd turned to ask the woman. He didn't know how the children's father would even know where they were unless Barbara had told him.

"He had a picture and he said he was their father," Lizette said. "He had a snake on his arm."

Amanda went still in Judd's arm. The kids had told him about the snake.

Judd nodded. He should have figured something like

this would happen. He wondered if his cousin had gotten back with her husband, after all. Generally, Judd was a supporter of married folks staying together. But some of the things Bobby had let slip while he was at Judd's place would make anyone advise Barbara to forget her husband.

The one thing Judd knew was that he didn't want that man to come within shouting distance of the children.

"You have a lock on this place, I suppose," Judd said as he looked inside the building the woman was going to use for her school. If he brought the kids to the lessons and then came back to pick them up, they should be safe.

"I could put a lock on," one of the older men spoke up. "It's no trouble. They have some heavy-duty ones over at the hardware store."

"And it wouldn't hurt Charley here to come over and sit while the kids have their lessons," another older man offered. "He always complains that the chairs at the hardware store are too hard anyway. Now that he's got his fancy phone, he can call the sheriff any time, night or day."

Judd nodded. It felt good to have neighbors, even if he hadn't been very neighborly himself. He wasn't sure what he could do to repay them, but he intended to try. "I'll be watching, too."

"Is something wrong?" Lizette looked at the men's faces.

"Their father isn't fit to be near these kids—even the court says so," Judd said quietly. He could see the alarm grow on Lizette's face. "Not that you have to worry about it. We'll take care of the guarding. You won't even know we're here. We can even sit outside."

"In the snow?" Charley protested.

"Of course you can't sit outside in the cold," Lizette said. "I'll put some chairs along the side of the practice area. And I'll be careful about who else I accept as students. I'll check references on any grown man who wants to join the class."

Charley snorted. "Ain't no grown man hereabouts that'll sign up. Not if he wants to keep his boots—"

One of the other older men interrupted him. "I thought you was gonna sign up yourself, Charley. You can't just sit and watch everyone else practice. That wouldn't be right."

"Why, I can't do no ballet," Charley said, and then looked around at the faces of his friends. "I got me that stiff knee, remember—from the time I was loading that heifer and it pinned me against the corral?"

"The exercises might even help you then," Lizette said. "We do a lot of stretching and bending to warm up."

If Judd hadn't still been thinking about the children's father, he would have laughed at Charley's trapped expression. As it was, he was just glad Charley would be inside with the children. For himself, Judd thought, he'd set up a chair outside the door, so he could keep his eyes on who was driving into Dry Creek.

Judd didn't trust the children's father and was determined to keep the man as far away from Dry Creek as possible. First thing in the morning Judd decided he'd tell Sheriff Wall all about the court order.

Judd had only met the sheriff once, but he trusted the man. Sheriff Wall might not be one of those big-city sheriffs who solved complicated crimes, but he had the persistence and instincts of a guard dog. And the man knew every road coming near Dry Creek, even the ones that were just pasture trails. The kids would be safer with Sheriff Wall on the job.

"I can pay in advance for the lessons," Judd announced. He didn't like the sympathetic look the ballet woman was giving the kids now that Charley had accepted his fate. Judd didn't want the woman to think they couldn't pay their way, especially not when she'd have to give special attention to the security of her classroom.

"There's no need to pay now," the woman protested.

But Judd already had two twenty-dollar bills in his hand and he held them out to her. "Let me know if it costs more."

"That should cover their first couple of lessons," Lizette said as she took the money and turned to a desk in a corner of the large room. "Just let me get a receipt for you."

Judd watched the woman walk over to the desk. He couldn't help but notice that she didn't just walk—she actually glided. He supposed that was what all of that ballet did for a body.

Judd tried not to gawk at the woman. The fact that she moved like poetry in motion was no excuse for staring at her.

Judd heard a soft collective sigh and turned to see all the old men watching the woman as if they'd never seen anyone like her before. Charley had obviously forgotten all about his reluctance to be in the class.

"There's no need for a receipt," Judd said.

The woman looked up from the desk. Even from across the room he could see she was relieved. "But you should have one anyway. Just as soon as I get all my desk things organized, I'll see that you get one. I could mail it to you, if you leave me your address."

"I'm at the Jenkins place south of town. Just write *Jenkins* on the envelope and leave it on the counter in the hardware store."

It had taken Judd two weeks to figure out the mail system in town. The first part was simple. The mail carrier left all of the Dry Creek mail at the hardware store, and the ranchers picked it up when they came into town. The second part still had Judd confused. For some reason, if he wanted to get his mail sooner rather than later, he still had to have it addressed to the Jenkins place even though no one by the name of Jenkins had lived on the ranch for two years now.

When Judd finally bought the Jenkins place, he told himself he'd get the name changed. He'd asked the mail carrier about it, and the man had just looked at him blankly and said that's what everyone called the place.

Judd vowed that once he had the children taken care of and the deed to the place signed, he'd take a one-page ad out in that Billings paper everyone around here read. He'd make sure people knew it wasn't the Jenkins place anymore.

But, in the meantime, he didn't want to have the woman's envelope returned to her, so he'd go along with saying he lived at the Jenkins place.

The woman nodded. "I know about the hardware store. I've been meaning to post an announcement about the school so everyone will know that we're currently taking students."

"About the students—" one of the old men said and then cleared his throat. "You see, the students—well, we're not sure how many students you'll have."

"Of course," Lizette assured him. She knew she needed a few more students to do the ballet, but surely three or four more would come. "No one knows how many people will answer the flyer I put up. But I need to start the classes anyway if we're going to perform the Nutcracker ballet before Christmas."

Lizette figured the students who came later could do the parts that involved less practice.

"Christmas is only five weeks away," Judd said and frowned. He knew when Christmas was coming because he figured his cousin would surely come for the children before Christmas.

Judd had gone ahead and ordered toys for the kids when he'd put in a catalog order last week, but he thought he'd be sending the presents along with them when their mother picked them up. Thanksgiving was next week, and it was likely the only holiday he'd have to worry about. He figured he could cope with a turkey if he could get Linda to give him some more basic instructions. She'd already told him about some cooking bag that practically guaranteed success with a turkey.

"I don't suppose you have a real nutcracker in that ballet?" one of the older men asked hopefully. "I wouldn't say no to some chopped walnuts—especially if they were on some maple doughnuts."

"You know there's no doughnuts, so there's no point in going on about them," Charley said firmly as he frowned at the man who had spoken. "There's more to life than your stomach."

"But you like doughnuts, too," the older man protested. "You were hoping for some, too—just like me."

"Maybe at first," Charley admitted. "But I can't be eating doughnuts if I'm going to learn this here ballet."

Lizette smiled as she looked at the two men. "Well, I do generally make some sort of cookies or something for the students to eat after we practice. I guess I could make doughnuts one of these days."

"You mean you can bake doughnuts?" Charley asked. "I didn't know anyone around here could bake doughnuts."

Lizette nodded. "I'll need to get a large Dutch oven, but I have a fry basket I can use."

"Hallelujah!" Charley beamed.

"And, of course, I'd need to have some spare time," Lizette added.

"And she's not likely to have any time to bake now that she's starting classes," Judd said, frowning. It would be harder to guard the kids if every stray man in the county was lined up at the ballet school eating doughnuts.

Judd told himself that it was only his concern for the safety of the kids that made him worry about who was likely to be visiting the ballet school. He'd been in Dry Creek long enough to know about all the cowboys on the outlying ranches.

A woman like Lizette Baker was bound to attract enough attention just being herself without adding doughnuts to the equation.

Not that, he reminded himself, it should matter to him how many men gawked at the ballet teacher. He certainly wasn't going to cause any awkwardness by being overly friendly himself. He was just hoping to get to know her a little better.

She was, after all, the kids' teacher, and he was, for the time being, their parent. He really was obligated to be somewhat friendly to her, wasn't he? It was his duty. He was as close to a PTA as Dry Creek had, since he was the almost-parent of the only two kids in her class right now. If Bobby and Amanda were still with him in a few months, he'd have to enroll them in the regular school in Miles City instead of homeschooling them. But, until then, it was practically his civic duty to be friendly to their ballet teacher. And he didn't need a doughnut to make him realize it.

Chapter Five

Lizette worried there was something wrong with her. She thought she had been working through the grief of her mother's death, but maybe she was wrong. After all, she hadn't had that much experience with mourning, and the chaplain at the hospital had talked about going through different stages of grief.

Lizette wondered if one of those stages of grief was twitching.

Here she was wrapping up the day's dance lesson, and her mind wasn't concentrated on the three people who were her students or the five more students she needed if she was going to pull off even a modified version of the Nutcracker ballet. Instead, she was all jumpy inside, and her gaze kept going to the window, where she could see Judd sitting on the steps of her school and looking out to the street with a scowl on his face.

If she didn't get a firm hold on herself, she'd be actually twitching when she looked at that man.

Lizette had had three days of lessons now, and for the better part of all of those days Judd had had his back turned toward her and the students. The first day she didn't notice his silence and his scowls. The second day she noticed, but she didn't feel the need to do anything about it. Today, she felt obsessed by the man.

She kept fighting the urge to go out and talk to him— and that was after she'd already been outside five times today to ask him questions. She didn't have much to talk about either, except for the weather, and how many times could she ask if it looked like it was going to snow? He'd think she was dim-witted. There wasn't even a cloud in the sky anymore.

She kept expecting each time she went out and asked the man a question that she would then be able to move on with her lessons with a focused mind.

She was still waiting for that to happen.

The really odd thing was that nothing had changed in those three days.

She didn't need to see his face to know he wore the same scowl he'd worn every day so far. Every time today she'd found an excuse to slip outside and ask him a question, she'd known he'd have the same fierce look on his face even before she opened the door.

Lizette wondered if Judd thought his look would

keep strange cars off the street in front of the school. Actually, he might be right about that one. That scowl of his would stop an army tank from approaching him.

With all of the frowning, Lizette knew there was no sane reason she should feel drawn to go up and talk to him. But she was.

She thought it might be his shoulders. For as hard as his face scowled, his shoulders told a different story. It wasn't anger he was feeling, but worry. Anxiety hung on his shoulders. It was there in the way he angled his head when he heard a sound and the way he stood to take a look down the road every half hour or so.

Judd was taking his duty seriously, and he was worried.

That's it, Lizette thought to herself in relief. She found him compelling because he was protecting the children. She'd just lost her mother, and the man was obviously doing everything he could to guard the children in his care. That made him an unconscious picture to her of her mother, she told herself. She'd be as attracted to a chicken if it sat there guarding its eggs. It had nothing to do with the fact that he was a man. He was simply a concerned parent.

Lizette felt better having figured that out. Not that she would have been opposed to finding the man attractive as a *man*, she just didn't have time for that kind of distraction right now. She only had three students—

Amanda, Bobby and Charley. She needed to worry about getting more students instead of thinking about some man's shoulders.

And, yet, she let herself walk over to the doorway. Bobby and Amanda were sitting on the wooden floor untying their dance shoes. Since Charley wore socks instead of dance shoes, he didn't have to worry about ties. Instead, he was pulling in his stomach and admiring himself in the mirror she'd hung behind the exercise bar. None of her students needed her immediate attention.

"They're almost done," Lizette said as she walked out on the porch and crossed her arms in the chill. At least she wasn't asking about snow this time, even though the air felt cold enough for it. She always wore black tights and a black wrap-around dress when she practiced. Unfortunately, the dress was sleeveless. "Aren't you cold out here waiting for the kids?"

Judd looked up at Lizette and forgot to frown. He almost forgot to breathe. She was standing in front of the sun, and although the temperature was low enough outside to make his fingers ache if he didn't keep them in his pockets, the sun was shining brightly and she looked as though she was rimmed with gold. Her black hair was pulled back into a bun, and the smooth lines of her head made him think of an exotic princess. Her face was smooth and, even without lipstick, she looked like a picture he'd once seen of Cleopatra. The flimsy black thing she had draped over her made her look as if she was in constant motion. No wonder there had been so many wars fought back in Cleopatra's day.

Judd was outclassed and he had sense enough to know it. All he asked was that he not embarrass himself around her. "It's not that cold. Forty-six, last I checked."

"Yes, well." Lizette smiled.

"And no snow," Judd added.

He'd already figured out that it wasn't snow she was worried about. The few clouds that had been in the sky this morning were long gone. No, it was the kids' father she was fretting about. She didn't know Judd well enough to know that she didn't have to worry about him leaving his post.

Not that he minded her coming out to check on him. He knew he hadn't been around many women in his life, but he didn't remember women being this naturally beautiful. He almost smiled in return. "So the kids are almost finished? Did they do all right?"

Lizette smiled even wider. "You do make a good mother."

"What?" Judd choked on the smile that didn't happen. Had he heard her right? She thought he made a good *mother?* A mother?

"I mean with all of your concern and all," Lizette continued.

Judd grunted. He'd known he was out of her class, but he hadn't realized he was that far out of it. A man didn't get further away from date material than having a woman think of him as a mother.

"I used to ride rodeo." Judd thought he owed it to himself to speak up. "Won my share of ribbons, too. Bronc riding and steer wrestling. They're not easy events. I placed first in 2003 in bronc riding at the state fair in Great Falls."

"Is that where you got your scar?"

Judd had forgotten he had a scar on the right side of his forehead. The scar hadn't made any difference to his life, and he no longer even really saw it when he shaved. "No, I got that in a fight."

Judd didn't add that it had been a snowball fight when he was eight years old. He'd been dodging a snowball and hadn't seen the low-hanging branch of the tree. He wasn't going to admit he had got the scar playing, however—not when he was talking to a woman who thought of him as a mother.

"I'll bet you're strong," Lizette said, and almost shook herself. That was the most obvious come-hither line a woman had ever uttered, and she felt foolish saying it. Unfortunately, it either wasn't obvious enough for Judd, or he was just not interested. It didn't even make his scowl go away. "I mean, of course you're strong. You'd have to be with the way you swing Amanda around."

Lizette had watched the way Amanda ran to Judd after classes. The little girl would run straight at him, and he'd bend down to scoop her up. While Amanda giggled, he'd gently toss her up in the air.

"You don't need to worry about Amanda and Bobby's father. I can take him in a fight if need be," Judd said. He figured that was what all the talk about how strong he was came from.

Neither one of them heard the two kids come out on the porch.

"He has a gun—my dad does," Bobby said.

"You don't need to worry about your father either," Judd said gently as he put his hand on the boy's head.

It had taken Judd a full month to calm the nightmares that woke Bobby up. The boy still wanted to sleep in a cot at the bottom of Judd's bed. Judd had figured he might as well let him, since Amanda was already sleeping on a cot on the right side of his bed. If he wasn't worried about them rolling out of his bed, Judd would have let the two children share it, and he would have rolled his sleeping bag out on the floor. But the cots were closer to the floor, and the kids seemed to like them.

"But if he has a gun," Lizette said, "shouldn't we let the sheriff know?"

"The sheriff already knows."

Judd had given a complete report. He had even given

the sheriff a photo of the kids' father that had been in one of the suitcases Barbara left with them.

That photo had given Judd many an uneasy moment. The photo was a picture of the two children, Barbara and her husband. He knew it had been taken a couple of years ago because a date was handwritten at the bottom of the picture. It had been one of those pictures from a photo booth like the kind you find in an amusement park. Judd had a feeling the family didn't have many photos. The fact that Barbara had left it for the kids might mean she knew she wasn't coming back.

But, right now, the photo was the least of his worries. Judd didn't like the pale look of both of the kids' faces. Of course, that might be because they were outside without their mittens on.

"Where'd you put your mittens?" Judd asked them as he stood up and herded the two children back into the warm room. He'd ordered the mittens from the back of the seed catalog, and he'd since wished he'd gotten three pairs for each of them instead of only two.

"I'm afraid that might be my fault," Lizette said as she followed them inside and closed the door behind herself. "I told them they could have a doughnut after class today."

"We didn't want to get our mittens dirty," Bobby explained. "The doughnuts have sugar on them."

"You don't need to give them doughnuts," Judd said,

even though he could smell the doughnuts and didn't blame the kids for leaving their mittens off. The ballet practice room smelled of home. The only smell they usually had in his kitchen was the aroma of his morning coffee. Everything else was canned or microwaved or put between slices of bread in a sandwich. Judd didn't know much about cooking, and he'd never met anyone who actually baked. Even Linda at the café didn't do that kind of baking.

"Of course she needs to give us doughnuts." Charley joined them from his perch on one of the chairs spaced around a work table. "I had to drive up to the Elkton ranch to borrow that Dutch oven. I would have driven further for homemade doughnuts. I mean to have one if it's offered."

"Did anyone see you borrow the Dutch oven?" Jake asked.

"Of course they saw me!" Charley said indignantly. "I didn't steal it."

"I mean, did any of the ranch hands see you borrow it? Or did you just talk to the cook?"

"Pete Denning saw me. He told the cook not to give it to me—said I'd be using the thing to soak my feet! I told him we were using it to make doughnuts."

Jake's worse fears were confirmed. "I don't suppose you told him the doughnuts weren't going to be anything more exciting than flapjacks."

"Now, why would I do that?"

"To avoid a stampede."

"Oh," Charley said as he considered the matter. "I didn't think of that."

Both men looked down the road.

"I don't see anyone though," Charley said. "Maybe Pete forgot."

"Not likely."

"Maybe we should eat our doughnuts now," Bobby said. He'd been standing beside Judd.

"And I'm sure you don't need to worry about someone else coming for doughnuts," Lizette added. "There are plenty of doughnuts to share with a few other people."

Judd grunted. Maybe they were all right. Maybe he didn't need to worry about a stampede of cowboys coming for doughnuts. They probably thought Charley was doing the cooking anyway, and Charley wasn't known for his skills in the kitchen.

Lizette came back with a platter of doughnuts and some white paper napkins. There were powdered doughnuts and maple doughnuts. Twisted cruller doughnuts and apple doughnuts. Even jelly doughnuts.

Lizette tucked a napkin into the neckline of Amanda's dress and then put one into Bobby's shirt before spreading white napkins on the table in front of each of them.

"You made these?" Judd asked. He felt as wide-eyed as those cowboys he was worried about. He knew Lizette had said she made doughnuts, but he'd never expected that she could make doughnuts like these. He'd expected something more like biscuits. But these doughnuts were so perfect they glistened.

"I used to work in a bakery," Lizette said as she held the platter out to Charley. "Part of that time as a baker."

"There must be two dozen doughnuts here," the older man marveled as he took a jelly doughnut and eyed the rest longingly. "Maybe three dozen."

"Well, if you're making doughnuts, you can't just make a few." Lizette passed the platter to the children next. "The recipes all make about five dozen."

Amanda took an apple doughnut and Bobby took a maple one.

Judd was still standing, but Lizette turned the platter toward him anyway. "I know you're not a student, but you're working, too."

Lizette gave him a small, hopeful smile. Judd would have taken a burnt stick off a platter if she'd offered it to him with that smile. As it was, he picked up the first doughnut he touched—it was a cruller.

"Don't you need a machine or something to make doughnuts?" Judd said after he ate his first bite of pure heaven. "I didn't know regular people could even make doughnuts like these."

Lizette laughed. "All you really need is something to make the holes. Oh, and a Dutch oven, of course, unless you have a deep fryer."

Charley took a bite out of his doughnut and started to purr. "I could put in an extra practice session this afternoon if you want."

"I don't think that will be necessary," Lizette said. "But if that's a hint that you'd like a second doughnut, you can have one anyway."

"Ah, well, then," Charley said as he took another bite out of his doughnut. "Too bad the boys over at the hardware store don't know you're giving these to your students. They'd be signed up in no time."

Judd stopped eating his doughnut. He'd just looked out the window and had seen several of the ranch hands from the Elkton place go into the hardware store. He supposed it was too optimistic to think they'd come to town to buy nails.

"Well, I could take the tray over to the hardware store," Lizette said as she looked out the window in her studio and into the big window in the hardware store. "We certainly won't be able to eat all of these doughnuts, and we do need a few more dancers to do the Nutcracker."

"Jacob would appreciate a doughnut," Charley said. "He's been eating his own cooking for weeks now."

"Why don't you go get Jacob and invite him over,"

Judd suggested. So far the hardware store door was still shut. Maybe the cowboys really had come in for nails. "Just don't tell him there's doughnuts here."

"I know how to keep a secret," Charley said as he slowly stood up. "Although the pastor might want a doughnut, too, and I wouldn't feel right overlooking those two little boys of his if they're there."

"Oh, please invite the children," Lizette said. "I heard the pastor had two boys. I just haven't had a chance to invite them to ballet class yet."

"I'm not sure you'll want them in your class," Charley said doubtfully. "They have a tendency to be hard on the furniture."

"That's perfect then, because I don't have any furniture—at least not in the practice area," Lizette said. So far she had just fixed up the main room in her building. The building had been a grocery store years ago, and it had a nice backroom with a kitchen area that she was using as a small apartment for herself. "And if they're the kind of boys that like to move a lot, I'll just make them be mice."

Amanda giggled. "You can't turn boys into mice."

"Oh, yes, I can," Lizette said as she tousled Amanda's hair. "If I can turn a little girl into the Sugar Plum Fairy, I can turn little boys into mice or snowflakes or flowers."

"I'd rather be a mouse than a flower," Bobby said.

"Well, we'll see," Lizette said as her hand rested on Bobby's head, too. "Maybe you can even be something more exciting than either one."

Judd wasn't so sure about Lizette's powers to turn little boys into mice, but watching her casual affection with the children sure turned him into something else.

"I'm surprised you don't have children," Judd said. "Of your own, I mean."

Lizette looked up at him. "I do hope to have children some day."

Judd could only nod. He didn't really even have any good reason to feel so disappointed. Of course she wanted children. She had to be ten years younger than him, which would only make her twenty-three or twenty-four. A woman like her would want the whole family thing.

Judd didn't know where the thought had come from in the past few days that maybe he could marry if he just limited himself to a wife and didn't think of children. Children were what made a family anyway. He wouldn't have a clue about how to be a father. Sure, he'd gotten along fine with Bobby and Amanda. But they weren't like other kids. They'd been frightened so badly that they clung to him for safety. If he hadn't been there, they would have clung to that stray dog of his as long as the dog defended them from their nightmares.

Other children would expect more. No, a man like

him had no business thinking about raising children. Maybe someday he'd meet a woman who didn't want to have children either, and the two of them could marry.

Suddenly the doughnut Judd was eating didn't taste so good. It was too bad about Lizette.

Chapter Six

Lizette heard the sound of boots crunching in the snow. Lots of boots.

"Better hide those doughnuts," Charley said as he stood and looked out the window. "Another couple of pickups from the Elkton ranch are parked in front of the hardware store. Wonder when they got here."

"It's too late," Judd said. He'd eaten the last of his doughnut, and he pushed his chair away from the table.

The door to the ballet school was closed, and there were a dozen knocks on it all at the same time. Lizette could see, just by looking out the side window, that a lot of men were standing on her porch.

"I don't suppose they want to sign up for class," Lizette said as she stood to go to the door.

"No, I can't imagine they want to be mice," Judd agreed.

Lizette looked over her shoulder at the platter of doughnuts she had on the table. It still had five doughnuts on it. She had the rest of the doughnuts in the back room.

She opened the door and saw a sea of cowboy hats nod at her. "Come in."

"Thank you, ma'am," the man who stepped over the threshold first said.

"My, it does smell like heaven in here," the second man said as he walked into the room.

Each man who stepped into the room craned his neck to see the doughnuts sitting on the platter that was on the table. There was a black mat next to the door, but none of the ranch hands paused to let their wet feet dry there.

"We just stopped by to say a neighborly hello," one of the cowboys said as he craned his neck to look around her at the doughnuts.

"That's nice," Lizette said. She decided that if they didn't notice her standing there, it was futile to point out the black mat. Besides, the mat wouldn't make much difference. If a couple of men stopped to let their boots dry, the others would just keep the door open and the floor would eventually get wet anyway. In addition, the air in the room would be cold.

"The doughnuts are for the ballet students," Charley said before anyone could carry the conversation further.

Then he sat back down at the table. "And for the men who have been guarding the school, of course."

Several of the older men stepped forward through the pack of cowboys.

"We're the guards," Jacob said as he stepped forward. Two other older men followed him. "We've been keeping a watch out the windows for strangers."

"That ain't a fair way to decide who gets the doughnuts—they haven't had to do anything but sit where they always sit," one of the cowboys said before he turned to Lizette and swept off his hat. "Begging your pardon, miss. I don't think I've had the pleasure of meeting you. My name's Pete Denning. The boys and I heard you were making doughnuts. What a fine thing to do on such a nice day."

Judd could see that the longer Pete talked to Lizette, the less concerned he'd become about the doughnuts. By the time the man had stopped introducing himself, he had a grin on his face that Judd would wager had nothing to do with baked goods.

"Of course, I'm not asking for any doughnuts for myself," Pete continued, confirming Judd's suspicions. "I just wanted to come over and see if I could do any chores for you—you know, something to welcome you to Dry Creek."

Judd grunted. "She's probably got some dishes to wash now that she's made the doughnuts."

Pete's smile wavered. "I was thinking more along the lines of chopping firewood or something. You know, one of those chores that single women need a man to help them out with."

"I have an electric stove," Lizette said. "And the dishes are all done. All I need is someone to dance for me."

Pete's smile brightened. "I can do that."

"She means the ballet," Charley muttered from where he sat at the table. "She's not talking about line dancing or anything fun."

"She's not?" Pete looked at Lizette. "You're sure? There's a place in Miles City that sets up a mean line dance."

"What place is that?" Jacob asked as he joined Charley at the table. "You're not thinking of the senior center, are you?"

"No, I'm not thinking of the senior center. How romantic would that be? No, I've got my own kind of places," Pete said.

"In Miles City?" Charley asked. "What kind of places are there that we don't all know about?"

There was a moment of tense silence.

"Thanksgiving is almost here, and that's no time for quarreling," Jacob finally said. "It's a time for lighting our candles at church instead." Jacob turned and addressed his words to Lizette. "That's been the tradition here since before the town started. Everyone lights a candle and says why they're grateful. It helps us all be thankful for what we've got."

"What we've got right now is doughnuts," one of the older men said as Lizette started passing the plate of doughnuts to the men who were the regulars in the hardware store. The man who spoke took a maple doughnut off the plate. "And I'm sure enough grateful for having one."

"I have more in back, so there's enough for everyone," Lizette said as the plate made its way around.

By now all of the cowboys were standing with their hats off. Lizette knew she should say something about going back to wipe their wet boots, but she didn't have the heart. They were all gazing at her with hope in their eyes, looking more like little boys than grown men.

Lizette went into the back room and brought out another full tray of doughnuts. She had a row of chocolate frosted ones, a row of powdered doughnuts, a few jelly ones, a row of apple ones and a section of maple bars. She'd even shaken red and green sprinkles over a couple of sugar-glazed doughnuts just to see what they'd look like when Christmas came. She was almost glad the ranch hands had stopped by. What would she have done with all of these doughnuts otherwise?

The men all sighed when Lizette carried the full tray over to where they stood.

"Of course, these doughnuts are to help advertise my ballet classes." Lizette felt she did owe it to herself to say that much as several hands reached for doughnuts. "And, remember, no one is too old for ballet."

One cowboy who was still reaching stopped with his hand midway to the doughnut. "We don't need to do this ballet stuff if we take one, do we?"

Another ranch hand who had already taken a bite of his doughnut sighed. "It would be worth it if we did."

"No, you don't need to sign up," Lizette said. Half of the doughnuts were already gone from the tray. She looked around and saw that everyone had a doughnut. "You could help by spreading the word though. We're hoping to do the Nutcracker ballet before Christmas, and I still need a minimum of five more students."

"The pastor has twin boys that are about six years old," Pete Denning said as he licked his fingers. He'd had a jelly doughnut from the plate earlier and was now eyeing the tray. "I think the pastor went to get them when we heard about the doughnuts."

"Well, we'll have to save some doughnuts for them then," Lizette said as she turned to take the tray out of the room.

"They might not want doughnuts," Pete said as he saw Lizette turn to leave.

Judd snorted. At least *he* knew kids better than that.

Pete heard him. "Well, maybe they'll want a doughnut, but their mother might not let them have one since it's so close to lunchtime and she'll be worried they won't eat their vegetables."

Judd flinched. He probably shouldn't have let Bobby and Amanda have doughnuts, either. This being a parent seemed to have lots of rules that he didn't know. He looked over at the two kids. They both had frosting on their chins and happy gleams in their eyes. It was likely they wouldn't want lunch.

Judd doubted the kids would eat any vegetables either if he put any in front of them at this point. He'd have to be sure they took a vitamin pill when they got home. He'd bought a big jar of children's vitamins when Bobby and Amanda first came. He didn't want his cousin to accuse him of stunting her kids' growth when she came to pick them up.

He wondered if he should take the kids to the dentist, too. When did kids start going to the dentist anyway?

Just then someone knocked on the door.

Lizette started to walk toward the door, but one of the ranch hands opened it before she got there.

Mrs. Hargrove came into the room and looked around with surprise showing on her face. Or at least what Judd could see of her face seemed to show surprise. The older woman had a red wool scarf wrapped around her neck, and she started to unwind it. She was wearing a long pink parka with a green gingham house-dress under it. Her gray hair was clipped back with a red barrette. Mrs. Hargrove was always colorful.

"You must have gotten the news then?" Mrs. Hargrove said as she looked around the room. She still stood on the small black mat that was beside the door. "Looks like I'm interrupting the celebration. Sheriff Wall always did say the rumor line beat the phone line in this part of the country any day."

"What news?" Judd asked since she seemed to be looking at him.

"They're just here for the doughnuts," Charley said as he jerked his head at the ranch hands. "They didn't bring anything but their appetites with them."

Mrs. Hargrove looked over at the group of cowboys and frowned. "Don't tell me you came to beg dough-nuts off of Lizette when she's hardly even settled in yet? What's she going to think of us?"

"Oh, that's all right," Lizette said. "I'd already made the doughnuts when they came."

"Still, these boys know better than to come in and eat up your food supplies like this. What if you were on short rations yourself?" Mrs. Hargrove looked at the men. "I'll bet each of you have been short a time or two in your lives."

"They're only doughnuts," Lizette said.

"No, she's right, Miss," Pete said as he pulled a dollar bill out of his pocket. "We sure don't expect you to feed us without getting something in return for it."

Pete put the dollar bill on the tray where the powdered doughnuts had been. He hadn't even finished putting the bill there before a dozen other bills joined the one he had placed there. She even saw a five dollar bill sticking out. There must be twenty dollars there.

"You really don't need to—" Lizette protested.

"We're happy to do it, Miss," Pete said. "Those were real fine doughnuts."

"The best I've ever eaten," another man said.

"I'd be willing to buy a whole tray of them if you want to make them," another man said. "It's my turn to bring something to eat when the guys get together on Friday night in the bunkhouse."

"Well, I guess I could make another batch," Lizette said. Now that she had the Dutch oven for the oil, all she would need was a few more eggs.

"I'll pay you a dollar a doughnut," the man said.

"Oh, that's too much," Lizette said. She could use the extra income, but she didn't want to overcharge her new neighbors. "Especially if you buy a few dozen."

"It's worth it to me, Miss," the man said. "Last time it was my turn to bring the dessert, I tried to make an angel food cake myself."

"It came out flatter than a pancake," another man said as he gave Lizette a pleading look. "You'd be doing us all a favor if you let him buy the doughnuts. We ended up eating crackers the last time he was in charge of refreshments. And even those were stale."

"Well, all right," Lizette said. "But you'll get a bulk discount on the price. How does eight dollars a dozen sound?"

Lizette knew that was somewhere between what a doughnut shop and a bakery would charge for a dozen doughnuts.

"You've got yourself a deal," the man said.

"So you don't know the news?" Mrs. Hargrove said now that she had unwound her scarf and finished scraping her shoes on the black mat. "About the—" Mrs. Hargrove stopped and looked at the children. "Well, the news will keep for a little bit I guess—what with the kids here."

"Are there some more kids who are going to be in the ballet?" Amanda asked Mrs. Hargrove. "We need more kids."

Judd watched as Mrs. Hargrove bent down until she was on the same eye level as Amanda. Judd could see why the older woman was such a popular Sunday-school teacher. She smiled at Amanda.

"I heard you're going to be the Sugar Plum Fairy," Mrs. Hargrove said.

Amanda's eyes shone as she nodded her head. "And I get to wear the fairy-princess dress. Want to see it?"

"Why don't you ask your teacher if you can bring it over and show it to me?" Mrs. Hargrove said.

Amanda ran over to talk to Lizette.

Judd wondered if Mrs. Hargrove was going to invite him to church again. He almost hoped so. He could use an excuse to talk with the older woman some more. She seemed to know all about children and she could probably answer some of his questions—like was Amanda too old to still suck her thumb occasionally and, even if she was, was it better to just let her be or should he try to do something about it?

He wondered what the news was that Mrs. Hargrove had come over to tell. Maybe she'd just heard that they were taking precautions to be sure the children's father didn't come near them. If that was it, he could put her mind at ease. "Jacob and Charley have been keeping the streets of Dry Creek safe. Well, technically, the *street* of Dry Creek."

There was just one main street that ran through the town.

"I understand you have been keeping watch, too," Mrs. Hargrove said with a nod to Judd. She then looked down at Bobby. "And I expect you have a little helper here."

Bobby smiled up at the woman. "We're guarding the ballet."

"So you're in the ballet, too," Mrs. Hargrove said

with an approving nod. "What part are you going to play?"

"I don't know yet. I might have to be a snowflake if we can't get any other kids to be in it with us."

"Ah," Mrs. Hargrove murmured. "Snowflakes are wonderful things. Especially at Christmas. Each one is different."

"Yes, ma'am," Bobby said without much enthusiasm.

"Why don't you go help your sister with that costume?" Judd said to Bobby. Judd had a feeling that Mrs. Hargrove wasn't going to tell him the news she had as long as either of the children were around to hear it.

Bobby pushed his chair back from the table and left to follow Amanda.

Mrs. Hargrove sat down in the chair Bobby had left. She didn't waste time but got straight to the point. "Have you heard from the sheriff this morning?"

Judd shook his head. "The kids have had lessons this morning, and I come in with them. I've been here."

"That's what the sheriff thought. That's why he called me. He wanted you to know that they think they've arrested the kids' father over in Miles City. The man won't say who he is, but he had that picture Lizette described with him."

"Did the man have a tattoo of a snake on his arm?"

Mrs. Hargrove nodded. "The sheriff said it was a cobra."

"That sounds like it's him, all right. Did he have a woman with him when he was arrested?"

Mrs. Hargrove shook her head. "No, it was just him. Are you thinking your cousin is hooked back up with him?"

"I don't know what to think," Judd admitted. "She should have been back here weeks ago, even if she'd had car trouble on the way to Denver. Besides, I don't know how he would know where to find the kids if he hadn't gotten the information from my cousin. Though I can't understand why she'd be foolish enough even to talk to the man."

"She must have had her reasons," Mrs. Hargrove said.

"Well, I hope they were good ones."

Mrs. Hargrove nodded. "The sheriff said they caught the man breaking into a gas station in the middle of the night."

"How long will he be in jail?"

"Long enough. They took him to the jail in Miles City for the time being. In a week or so they'll take him to the jail in Billings. If he is the children's father, apparently there's another warrant out for his arrest from the state of Colorado, so when they finish with him here, they're going to ship him down there."

"He's a popular guy."

"I'd say so. The sheriff figures they'll be sending him to Colorado sometime after Christmas."

Judd nodded. "That'll be some Christmas present for the kids."

Amanda and Bobby were starting to walk back toward them with the fairy costume in their hands. Even from here, Judd could see the excitement on Amanda's face.

"Do you think it will upset them to know their father's in jail?"

"I wish I knew," Judd said. "On the one hand, he is their father. But on the other hand, they're afraid of him. Knowing he's in jail might make them more comfortable even coming into town here. They seem a little nervous when they're not at my place."

Mrs. Hargrove nodded. "I wondered if that's why you haven't brought them to Sunday school yet." She didn't leave time for Judd to think of the real reason he hadn't brought the children. "But now that it's cleared up, I'll hope to see you this Sunday. It's the last Sunday before Thanksgiving, and the kids will be decorating candles and thinking about what they're going to say at the service we have the night of Thanksgiving."

"I heard about that—"

"It's a wonderful thing for families to do together,"

Mrs. Hargrove said as she turned to smile at Bobby and Amanda, who had just reached them.

Amanda was holding the pink costume out for Mrs. Hargrove to see.

"Oh, that's beautiful," Mrs. Hargrove told the little girl.

Watching Amanda talk with the older woman made Judd decide he would take the kids to Sunday school this Sunday. It would do Amanda good to talk to more people, and she certainly seemed to have no trouble chatting with Mrs. Hargrove. It would be good for Bobby, too, to meet some more kids.

The only one it might not be good for, Judd decided, was himself. He would be a fish out of water in church. Maybe he could leave the kids at the church and then walk over to the café and have a cup of coffee. Now that sounded like the way to do this. Although, now that he thought of it, he couldn't remember if the café was open on Sundays. He thought Linda went to the church in Dry Creek, too, so she probably didn't open the café that day.

For the first time, Judd wished Dry Creek were a bigger town. In a place like Billings, or even Miles City, no one would notice who was going to church and who wasn't. They probably had coffee shops that were open on Sunday mornings as well.

Maybe he'd just have to sit in his pickup for the hour or so that the kids were inside. Yeah, he could do that.

Chapter Seven

Judd still hadn't talked to the sheriff about it all, but it was Saturday, and it had been two days since Judd had learned that the kid's father had been arrested. Hearing that news had surprised Judd enough. But what he was looking at now made that surprise go clear out of his head. He figured pigs were going to start flying down the street of Dry Creek pretty soon. He couldn't believe his eyes. Right there, in the middle of Lizette's practice room, was Pete Denning trying to do a pirouette.

The man's Stetson hat was thrown on the floor, and his boots were next to it. He wore one white sock and one gray sock, but both of his feet were arched up in an effort to hold him on his tiptoes.

"We should start with something simpler," Lizette was saying. She was dressed in her usual black practice leggings and T-shirt and had stopped her stretching on the practice bar to watch Pete.

"No, I saw this on TV and I know I can do it," Pete said as he tried again to stand on his tiptoes.

The man looked like a pretzel that had come out of the machine wrong.

"I see you got another student," Judd said. The kids and Charley were in the other room getting out of their coats and into their dancing slippers. Judd should have positioned himself in his usual chair outside on the porch, but he'd seen Pete, and that had changed everything.

"It's a free country," Pete said.

Judd lifted his hands up in surrender. "I didn't say anything."

"Yeah, but I know what you're thinking."

Judd chanced a quick look at Lizette. She'd paused midway through a stretch, and the curve of her back was the most beautiful thing he'd ever seen. He certainly hoped the cowboy didn't know what he was thinking.

Pete didn't wait for Judd to answer. "You're thinking that a Montana man like me wouldn't know what to do with a little culture."

"I didn't say that."

"But you would be wrong even to think it," Pete continued without listening. Pete was looking at Lizette, too, now. Lizette had stopped bending and was stretching her arm along the practice bar. A faint sheen of perspiration made her face glow, and tiny wisps of black hair had escaped the braid she wore.

Pete sighed. "A true man can appreciate fine art."

Judd didn't like Pete looking at Lizette. The cowboy didn't have fine art on his mind. Judd knew that much at least.

"You might have to wear tights," Judd said. That got the other man's attention away from Lizette, so Judd added, "Pink tights."

Now he had the cowboy's full attention.

Pete wasn't looking at anyone but Judd. He looked horrified. "Nobody said anything about tights."

"I said there would be costumes," Lizette said as she lifted her leg onto the practice bar and made another curve with her body.

"But 'costumes' doesn't mean tights," Pete said as he watched Lizette.

For a moment, neither man spoke.

Pete breathed out slowly. "Well, maybe if they're not *pink* tights."

Lizette finished her ballet move and turned to look at the two men. "Don't discourage him, Judd."

Judd felt that odd sensation in his stomach again. The last day or so Lizette had started calling him Judd, and he liked the sound of his name coming from her lips. Of course, it *was* his name, so it shouldn't be any big deal. It was just that he wasn't used to people saying it all of the time. If he was on the phone with someone, he was usually called "Mr. Bowman." In the rodeo, people had just called him "Bowman." His uncle had called him "You," if he called him anything at all. Judd guessed first names were more of a woman's thing.

"I won't discourage him," Judd finally said. "I'm looking forward to seeing him prance around up on stage." He could see the panic return to the other man's eyes.

"If he backs out, Judd Bowman," Lizette warned. "You're going to have to take his place."

"Me? Up there?"

"It would do you good," Lizette said. "Especially if you scare away any of my students. I don't know what the phobia is about tights anyway. They're really no tighter than football uniforms."

"Yes, but with f-football—" Pete stuttered. "Well, with football, you get to knock people around."

"I'm hoping you're not going to say that that makes you more of a man than ballet does," Lizette said to Pete.

Judd felt a little sorry for the cowboy. The two of them both knew that, of course, football made a man more of a man. And real men wore boots and not ballet slippers. They just couldn't tell any of that to Lizette.

"No, ma'am," Pete finally said. "I'm not going to say that."

"Good, because I'm expecting three more new students today, and with any luck, we can start some serious practicing for the Nutcracker."

Judd almost groaned. He hoped she wasn't expecting three more of Pete's cowboy friends. He couldn't stay out on the porch with all of those cowboys in here practicing their moves. And he didn't know what excuse he would give Lizette for guarding her classroom from inside the room, especially now that they all knew the kids' father was in jail in Miles City.

"This Nutcracker you want me to play," Pete said. "Does the Nutcracker wear tights?"

Lizette smiled at the cowboy. "Usually, he does."

Pete nodded glumly. "The guy sounds like some kind of a nut all right." Another look of alarm crossed Pete's face. "He is a guy, isn't he?"

Lizette laughed. "Yes, he's a guy. He wears a tall red hat with a black band under the chin."

"And tights," Pete said.

"Yes."

Pete shook his head.

"I suppose if you insisted, you could be a snowflake. It's just that I was saving those parts for the little kids."

"Maybe I could be an usher," Pete offered. "They get to wear clothes, don't they?"

"Of course they wear clothes," Lizette said. "Everyone wears clothes. All dancers are fully clothed at all times. What made you think they weren't? I can't afford for that rumor to get around. I won't even keep the students I have if people hear that."

"Maybe you need some help with the scenery," Pete finally offered. "Something with hammering."

Judd watched the disappointment settle on Lizette's face.

"Charley has already offered to build the fireplace that we need. Mrs. Hargrove has offered us her artificial Christmas tree. And we won't have enough dancers to do even a small version of the Nutcracker if you back out now," Lizette said.

Judd was a fool. He just couldn't stand that look on Lizette's face. "I could do something."

"Charley already offered to build the fireplace," Lizette said.

"No, I mean, I could do a dance part."

Judd wished he'd offered sooner. Lizette looked at him like he'd just hung the stars in the sky.

"You would? Dance a part?"

"Now, just wait a minute," Pete said. "I haven't said I *won't* do any dancing. I was just offering some extra help. Besides, I thought the deal was that the first people to sign up got their pick of the parts. Isn't that why your little girl gets to be the Sugar Plum Fairy?"

Judd nodded. He guessed those were the rules.

"So I pick the meanest dancer in the whole thing," Pete said. "Someone who commands respect on the street. Is there a part like that?"

"Well, if you're sure you don't want to be the Nut-cracker, you can be the Mouse King," Lizette said, and then added quickly as Pete started to frown, "he's not a furry little mouse. He's really a rat. He comes charging out of the fireplace and tries to take down the Nut-cracker."

"Kind of like in football?" Pete said with a smile. "And I bet he doesn't have to wear tights."

"Well, he does usually wear tights," Lizette admitted. "But the rest of the costume covers them up pretty much."

"So Judd here's going to be the Nut guy?" Pete asked.

Lizette raised a hopeful eyebrow at Judd.

"I guess so," Judd admitted. He only hoped the Nut-cracker got to fight back when the Mouse King tack-led him. Judd didn't relish going down without a fight.

"Good," Pete said with satisfaction as he looked at Judd. "Let's hope that little black band keeps the hat on your head when I come after you."

Judd hoped the little black band kept his head on his shoulders when Pete tackled him. "This Nutcracker guy, he's not a coward or anything, is he?"

Judd had just realized he might be required to run away from Pete. He'd decided to make this little community his home, and he didn't want to get a reputation for running away from trouble.

"Oh, no, the Nutcracker fights him back," Lizette assured them both. "It's a glorious battle. All done in ballet, of course. The audience doesn't know until the last minute who wins."

Judd wondered how he was going to defend himself if he had to do it on tiptoes.

Just then the outside door to the dance classroom opened, and in walked Mrs. Hargrove and the pastor's twin boys.

"Well, we're here to learn to dance," Mrs. Hargrove said as Lizette moved to greet them.

Judd had to admit he was relieved. At least the new students weren't more cowboys.

"Oh, we're going to have such fun," Lizette said as she led Mrs. Hargrove and the twins back to the area where they could take off their coats.

Judd was less enthusiastic. His only consolation was that Pete didn't seem any happier about the arrangements than he was.

"I hope you've got room in those tights for some knee pads," Pete finally said, but he said it like the fight had already gone out of him. "I'd hate to bang up your knees too bad when I bring you down."

"My knees will do just fine," Judd said.

Pete was silent for a moment. "You don't suppose the guys are going to come to see this ballet thing, do you?"

Judd grunted. He figured there was about as much chance of the guys not coming to see this particular ballet production as there was of those pigs deciding to fly down the main street of Dry Creek. No, he and Pete were doomed to be everyone's merry entertainment for the holidays.

"You'd be welcome to come over to my place and hang out for a couple of days after the show if you want," Judd offered. He knew what a bunkhouse could be like when it came to teasing. "You could tell people you'd gone on a trip or something."

"I've been wanting to go to Hawaii."

"Well, maybe you could take that trip then. Winter's a slow time in ranching," Judd said.

"Can't afford to really go," Pete said.

"Well, then I'll just put some Hawaiian music on and turn up the heat in the spare room."

"I appreciate that," Pete said. "That doesn't mean I won't hit you hard when I can, but I do appreciate it."

Judd understood. Pete could no more take it easy on him than Judd could run away when Pete came after him. Even though Lizette had not told them how the fight turned out, Judd figured anyone who was named

King, even if it was Mouse King, was the one who won the battle. Judd supposed Pete figured it the same way; the cowboy sure didn't look worried that he'd lose.

When the rest of the dancers came back to begin practice, Judd and Pete were both ready. Judd wondered what kind of nonsense he'd let himself in for. But he was a man of his word, and one thing he knew for sure—Lizette was counting on him to dance a part. His might not be the best part in the whole ballet, but it was the part she needed and he was willing to play it for her.

Judd only hoped Lizette thought he was doing it for the kids. He wouldn't want her to know he'd taken one look at her disappointed face and agreed to make a fool of himself. No, a man had to have some pride, even if he was a nutcracker.

Chapter Eight

Judd ached. It was Sunday morning, and he'd gotten the kids up and dressed for Sunday school like he'd promised them, but his body ached all over. Just a few months ago, he'd loaded two tons of hay bales by hand with nothing more than leather gloves and a metal hook. He hadn't felt a single ache in his body then. He was a man in the prime of his life. He was a rancher. But one day of ballet practice had about done him in.

And they hadn't even started practicing their parts yet. Lizette had just shown them some basic ballet steps. She said she was going to wait to practice the individual steps when she got the costumes she was borrowing from her old teacher and made sure they all fit.

Lizette had taken a moment to tell both Judd and Pete that she was sure both of their costumes would fit. And if not, she said, she'd improvise. Judd figured it was her way of telling them they had no hope of escaping.

After about an hour of ballet practice, Judd had stopped worrying about wearing tights. He didn't care what he wore. He just hoped that the Nutcracker guy stood in one place and let the Mouse King plow into him. His body would hurt less that way than if he had to keep practicing.

"Can you braid my hair?" Amanda stood in front of him after breakfast with a blue ribbon in her hand.

"Oh, but it'll look pretty if we just brush it and tie the ribbon around it," Judd said. He'd never braided hair in his life.

"No, I want it to look like Miss Lizette's," Amanda said. "She's awfully pretty."

"That she is, sweetheart," Judd said as he picked up the ribbon. He supposed he could try to braid hair. He was good at tying knots; he should be able to figure out hair braids.

Judd did a cross between a sailor's knot and a square knot.

"It doesn't look like Miss Lizette's," Amanda said as she stood up to look in the driver's mirror of his pickup. Judd had just pulled into a parking place near the church and was unfastening the seatbelts the children wore.

"The ribbon's pretty," Judd said reassuringly.

Judd looked at the braid again. Amanda was right. It didn't look at all like the one Lizette wore. "Maybe if you keep your head tilted to the right."

Judd wondered how many times he needed to bring the kids to Sunday school before he could throw himself on the mercy of Mrs. Hargrove. If he could just spend an afternoon with her asking questions, he knew he could do a better job with Amanda and Bobby. There should be some kind of a book or something that people could buy when they inherited kids all of a sudden like he had. Something that covered nightmares and braids and the other questions he had.

"You're coming with us, aren't you?" Bobby asked anxiously after he and Amanda had both climbed out of the passenger side of the pickup.

Judd looked over at them. They looked like little refugee children, frightened of a new experience and excited all at the same time. They'd asked so many questions this morning about church and Sunday school that he knew they'd never gone to either in their short lives. They didn't know what to expect any more than he did.

"Sure. I'm coming," Judd said as he opened his door. He hoped this wasn't one of those churches that required ties, because he didn't own one. It had always seemed pointless to have a tie when he didn't have a suit. Judd wished he'd screwed up his courage and visited this little church before the children came. At least then he could tell them what it looked like inside.

"It might have windows with pictures," Judd had said this morning. He couldn't remember actually looking that closely at the church in Dry Creek, but churches had those stained-glass windows, didn't they?

Judd looked down the side of the church now. He didn't see any stained-glass windows showing from the outside. "Even if there's no pictures, Mrs. Hargrove will be there."

The last seemed to reassure Bobby and Amanda. Judd wished he had thought to remind them of that fact earlier.

"She's going to be the Snow Queen," Amanda said. "But her costume won't be as pretty as mine."

"I think you're going to have the prettiest costume of all," Judd agreed as they started walking up the steps of the church. He put his hand on top of Amanda's head.

"There's Miss Lizette," Amanda said when they reached the bottom of the steps.

Judd looked down the street. Sure enough, Lizette was walking toward them. She wore a red wool coat and had a small black hat on her head. She looked more uptown than anything Judd had ever seen in Dry Creek.

"Good morning," Judd said. He couldn't think of one good reason why he'd never bought a suit and a tie in his life. A man should be prepared for days like this.

"Hello," Lizette said as she smiled at them. "Are you going to church, too?"

Amanda nodded. "And we're going to sit in a pew," Amanda leaned over and confided to Lizette. "But that's not a stinky thing. Cousin Judd says it's a long chair and we've got to share it."

Judd figured even a tie wouldn't save him now. "The children were curious about church."

"Of course," Lizette said.

All four of them had come to a stop at the bottom of the church stairs. There were only seven steps to the landing, but Judd didn't feel inclined to step forward and, apparently, neither did anyone else.

"Have you been to church here before?" Lizette finally asked as she stood looking up at the door.

It was a perfectly ordinary door, Judd decided. A good solid-wood double door. It was winter so the door wasn't wide open, but it was open a good six inches or so and he could hear the sounds of people talking inside.

"No, I've never been," Judd admitted.

"Oh," Lizette said, and then looked at him instead of the door. "But you've been to other churches, right?"

Judd shook his head. "I don't know a thing about them."

"Me neither," Lizette said.

"I thought I should bring the children," Judd finally said.

Both Judd and Lizette looked down at the children and then looked at each other.

Lizette nodded. "Yes, the children should go to church."

Lizette held out her hand to Amanda. Judd held out his hand to Bobby. The four of them walked into church just like they were a family.

Yes, Judd thought. The next time he went to Billings he was definitely going to buy himself a suit and a tie.

Lizette looked around the church the minute she and Amanda stepped through the door. She'd searched through her costume trunk to find the French fedora she wore, and not another man or woman in the church was wearing a hat. She'd tried so hard to blend in that she was sticking out.

"Well, welcome," Mrs. Hargrove said as she walked over from another group of people. She had her hand extended out to Lizette. "I can't tell you how happy I am that you decided to join us this morning."

"I thought the children should come to church," Lizette said, and then blushed. She wasn't the one who was related to the children. It wasn't her place to see that they went to church.

"Oh, we have something for all ages," Mrs. Hargrove said as she extended her hand to Judd as well. "And you made it, too. I'm so glad."

Judd nodded.

"The children are going to decorate candles this morning," Mrs. Hargrove said as she leaned down to the level of Amanda and Bobby. "And you're going to talk about the light of the world."

"Can I make a blue candle?" Amanda asked. "I like blue."

"They have all colors of candles and sequins and all kinds of things to put on them," Mrs. Hargrove said as she motioned for another woman to come over. "Glory Curtis, the pastor's wife, will take you back to the Sunday-school room and get you settled."

Lizette watched the two children walk away with the pastor's wife.

"I can just wait outside until—" Judd began.

"Nonsense," Mrs. Hargrove said as she took them both by the arm. "The pastor has an adult Sunday-school class, and today's topic is how to have a happy marriage."

"Oh, but I'm not—" Lizette began.

"Nonsense," Mrs. Hargrove said as she walked them forward. "What he's going to say will apply to many relationships in life."

Judd decided that Mrs. Hargrove was wrong within five minutes of the pastor starting to talk. Judd had never had a relationship in his life that sounded like what the pastor described. His uncle certainly hadn't acted that way toward him. He'd never had a friend who was like that. Certainly none of the women he'd met on the rodeo circuits had cared about him that way.

He'd never even heard things like the pastor read from the Bible. What kind of person did good things to the people who wanted to do bad things to them? That would be like if the Nutcracker guy just lay down and let the Mouse King dance all over him and then got up and thanked him for it. The world would be all lopsided if that kind of stuff started happening. A man could get all confused about who his enemies really were.

"Inspiring," was all Judd could think of to say when the pastor finished the lesson and came over to greet him and Lizette.

"Very inspiring," Lizette added.

The pastor chuckled. "I'll admit it doesn't make a whole lot of sense at first. The one thing you'll learn about God though is that He turns things upside down a lot."

Judd nodded. He wasn't sure he wanted to be standing here talking with the pastor about God. What he knew about God wouldn't fill an old lady's thimble, and he didn't want to appear ignorant in front of Lizette, especially not now that she'd taken his arm by the elbow. He doubted she even realized she was leaning into him a little. He liked the faint lilac perfume she was wearing. He wondered if it was okay to notice a woman's perfume in church. He supposed it was a sin. Of course, he couldn't ask. A man should already know something like that.

"We've got coffee out back in the kitchen," the pastor said. "We've got some tables set up, and you're welcome to sit and have a cup while you wait for the kids to finish. We'll be starting church services in about fifteen minutes."

Judd hadn't realized there was more to this church business than what he'd just sat through, but he wasn't about to say anything.

"I could use a cup of coffee," Lizette said.

The church kitchen was painted yellow and smelled like strong coffee. Mugs sat on the counter next to a big urn of coffee. Next to the coffee was another urn that held hot water. A basket of various tea bags sat next to the hot-water urn. Several card tables were set up on the wall opposite the cabinets. Folding chairs rested against the wall.

Judd and Lizette were the first ones in to get coffee. They both moved toward the urn as if they were dying of thirst.

"I don't belong here," Lizette burst out before she even got to the coffee mugs.

"*You* don't belong? I don't even have a tie," Judd muttered as he reached for a mug.

"Nobody here is wearing a tie—or a hat," Lizette

said. "There should be a book telling people what to expect in church."

"I guess they just assume most people know those things," Judd said as he held the mug. "Would you like coffee or tea?"

"Tea, please. And how would we know what to expect in church? I've never been to church before."

Judd turned to fill the mug with hot water. "When you say you've never been to church, you just mean recently, don't you? I mean, I know you had a mother and a reasonable family life—I thought all families went to church at some point."

"Not ours."

Judd handed Lizette the mug of hot water. "I'll let you pick the tea you want."

Lizette pulled a lemon spice packet out of the basket and tore the paper wrapping off the tea bag. She put the bag in the hot water. "My mother was always mad at God. I don't think she had ever heard about any of the kinds of things the pastor was talking about back there."

"I wonder if he knows what he's talking about," Judd said as he poured himself a cup of coffee. Then he flushed. He might not know much about church etiquette, but he was pretty sure a visitor wasn't supposed to call the pastor a liar. "I mean, maybe something is translated wrong."

Lizette nodded. "It is pretty odd, isn't it? But I imagine he knows what he's talking about. Mrs. Hargrove seems to trust him, and I noticed she carries a Bible around with her. She must read it and agree with the man."

Judd nodded as they both walked over to one of the card tables. He had a tendency to trust Mrs. Hargrove. "It just must be that church is one of those things people like me don't understand."

They both sat down.

"What do you mean by that?" Lizette had wrapped her hands around her cup of tea, but she was making no move to lift the cup and drink any of it. Her face looked serious.

Judd's heart stopped. Here he had been muttering to himself, never expecting anyone to listen. It looked like Lizette had been listening.

"You keep saying 'people like me' like you were raised on Mars or something," Lizette said with a smile. "You don't look that different to me."

Judd swallowed. There had to be a lot of clever things to say to that kind of question. Pete would know something brash to say that would turn the moment into a chuckle. But Judd realized he didn't want to avoid the question. "I'm different because I was raised by an uncle who didn't care about me. He never once celebrated my birthday. What am I saying? He never even said 'Good morning' or 'How was your day?' or 'Do you feel all right?' I could have laid down and died and he wouldn't have noticed except for the fact that the chores hadn't gotten done."

"Oh."

Judd plowed on. "I'm not saying that to say I had it worse than everyone else, it's just that I'm different. A lot of things other men know—things like how to be part of a family—those are things I don't know."

There. Judd had made his speech. It wasn't fancy, but it was the first time in his life he'd come out and said why he was so different.

"I do know how to work, though." Judd felt he needed to add something positive. "That's one thing I learned living with my uncle. I learned how to work."

"Oh."

Judd didn't add that he'd also learned not to trust anyone and not to expect anything from anyone else.

There was a moment of silence.

And then Lizette took a sip of tea. "My mother always wanted me to be a ballet dancer."

"But you *are* a ballet dancer."

"Yes, but don't you wonder what would have happened if I hadn't been able to dance?" Lizette asked. "What would have happened between my mother and me then? I think part of me always wondered about that, but I was afraid to ask her—I was even afraid to ask myself the question."

Judd had never thought that someone who had a family still might have had problems.

"Well," Judd said. He didn't know what else to say, so he just put his hand over Lizette's hand and patted it like he would have patted Amanda's hand if she had been there.

Judd guessed that maybe there was something to this going to church after all. Before he knew it, he wasn't patting Lizette's hand but was holding it instead.

"The tea's kind of hot," Lizette said as she blinked.

"Yeah, so is the coffee," Judd said as he pulled out a handkerchief and gave it to Lizette. He might not have a tie, but he'd started carrying one or two extra handkerchiefs since Amanda and Bobby had come into his life. It seemed like a lot of things were changing since those kids had come into his life.

Chapter Nine

Lizette wasn't ready for her students to come for practice. Oh, she was ready. She'd received the box of costumes and props from Madame Aprele and she had them laid out in the back room. She had the stage book marked for Charley, the narrator, so he could read aloud the abbreviated story of the Nutcracker and direct some of the scenes. What she wasn't ready for was to see Judd.

How did you explain to a man that you aren't crazy? Especially when he's seen your mood swing with his own eyes. She still didn't know what had happened. One minute, she was sitting there drinking tea with Judd and, before she knew it, she was sniffling into his handkerchief and talking about her mother. Lizette hadn't even known all of those questions about whether or not she measured up to her mother's hopes were inside her until they came spilling out to Judd. She was a mess.

It was the pastor's fault, of course. All of the talk about love and family and forgiveness—well, anyone would start to thinking about their life, wouldn't they?

It's just that it couldn't have happened at a worse time. She'd wanted to impress Judd. He was sort of the parent of the first two real students she'd ever had in her life, and she wanted him to see her as a professional.

After listening to her cry yesterday, he probably saw her as someone who *needed* a professional instead of someone who *was* a professional.

And he hadn't even had a choice but to listen to her. He'd patted her hand after her first few tears and told her that it would be all right. She should have stopped then. But she didn't. She'd gone on and on, telling him about this and that, and he'd kept patiently patting her hand. Then he'd held her hand for a bit, and it was the sweetest thing. Most men would have used the whole thing to make a move on a woman, but Judd didn't. Which, when Lizette thought about it, was the most embarrassing thing of all.

She'd been vulnerable and he'd been a gentleman. She'd been around enough to know what that meant— he wasn't interested. Plain and simple. No chemistry.

Not that she cared if he was interested. It was really best that he wasn't. After all, she was the teacher of the children under his care. He certainly wasn't obligated to think of her as anything but a teacher. She didn't *want* him to think of her as anything but a teacher.

And, to make things even worse, when it was all over and she'd cried her fill, he'd taken pity on her and asked her to sit with him and the children in church. Of course, she couldn't say no, because by then other people were coming in behind them for coffee, and she didn't want to turn around and have to face the others. So she had to keep sitting at the table with Judd until she'd blinked away some of the redness in her eyes.

In the meantime, Judd kept enough conversation going with the others so that no one noticed she wasn't turning around and talking. And he'd done it all so naturally, as though he was used to taking care of someone.

Lizette was never going to go to church again.

Judd wouldn't have believed that Lizette had cried in one of his handkerchiefs yesterday morning. Amanda had asked over breakfast if she could invite Lizette over for Thanksgiving dinner, and Judd had actually agreed it was a good idea. He'd thought they'd all had a nice time together yesterday. Now, he wasn't so sure. It was practice time for the ballet, and the woman whose soft hands he'd held yesterday had turned into a drill sergeant today, and she apparently saw him as nothing more than a raw recruit.

"I can march or I can ballet," he finally said. "I can't do both."

Well, Judd admitted, that was an exaggeration. He could march, but he wasn't so sure anyone could call his tortured steps ballet. People couldn't walk like that, could they? Lizette insisted she wasn't trying any advanced moves, but they sure seemed advanced to him.

Mrs. Hargrove and Charley were sitting on two folding chairs at the back of the practice room talking intensely until they both happened to look at him doing his ballet moves. Judd couldn't decide if it was encouragement or astonishment that he saw in their eyes, and he wasn't about to ask. At least they had stopped their conversation and bothered to look at him.

Which was more than he could say for Lizette. She didn't even look at him to see how he was doing when he complained. The only students she looked at this morning were the children. His sole consolation was that Pete looked even more bewildered than he was.

"My toes don't bend backward," Pete said.

"Of course not," Lizette said with some alarm in her voice as she left the children and went to Pete's side. "You must have your feet placed wrong. Here, let me help you."

Lizette put her arm around Pete and stood at his side. "Now, do this."

Judd grunted. Pete wasn't even looking at Lizette's feet as she showed him how to move his big feet. Instead, the cowboy was grinning triumphantly over at Judd. Well, Judd had to admit that the cowboy knew how to get a lady's attention better than he did even if he was just as bad at ballet.

"Now you try it," Lizette said to Pete.

"Ah." Pete looked around in alarm. "I think I need to see it all again."

"You put your foot like this," Lizette began again.

Judd wondered why she needed to keep her arm around the cowboy when all she was doing was showing him how to stand on his tiptoes. "Shouldn't he be practicing at the bar over there?"

Judd knew the bar was for practicing. He didn't much like looking in the big mirror behind the bar, but he did know what it was for.

"I'm learning just fine here," Pete said. "It's not easy being a rat."

Judd grunted. He thought the other man was doing a particularly fine job of being a rat.

"I think a rat would move his feet like this," Pete said as he danced a little.

Fine, Judd thought, now the cowboy was doing interpretive dance.

"That looks a little like the tango," Lizette said with a frown. "That's good, but it's more like the steps the mice would take. You're the leader. You need more power in your moves. You play a huge king rat."

"Think big and fat," Judd offered. "All of that cholesterol from the cheese."

Pete scowled at him. "I'm sure I'm a very fit rat."

"I don't see you eating any cottage cheese in this role," Judd said. If anyone should have power in their moves, it should be the Nutcracker. Judd had a feeling he was going to need some power.

"At least no one's going to be staring at my legs like they will be at the Nutcracker's," Pete said smugly. "I have a costume that covers my legs."

"Oh, that's right," Lizette said. She moved away from Pete and stood in the middle of the room. "Let's take a break and try on the costumes. Then we'll do a quick read through with the narration so people get familiar with the story. We'll do the actions, but not worry about all of the dance steps yet."

"Good." Judd could do action.

The children and Pete went into the back room first to look at the costumes. Judd wanted to talk with Mrs. Hargrove.

"Good morning," Judd said as he walked over to her and sat down in the chair that Charley had just vacated.

Charley decided to go into the back room to see the costumes, too.

Mrs. Hargrove smiled and nodded. Then she waited.

"I enjoyed church yesterday," Judd lied. It was true that he'd found church very interesting, but he could hardly say that. It made the whole experience sound scientific and cold, and it hadn't been, either. Lizette had been right that there should be some advice book about churchgoing.

"I thought you might think it was a bit too personal," Mrs. Hargrove said.

"Oh, no," Judd lied again. Now that he thought about it, that was exactly what had been wrong with all those things the pastor was saying. Whose business was it anyway how he wanted to treat his enemies? Enemies shouldn't expect nice treatment. Maybe people wouldn't have so many enemies if everyone just stayed with their own business.

"I'm glad you feel that way," Mrs. Hargrove said. "I'll look for you to become a regular at church then."

"Ah," Judd stammered. He didn't want to give that impression. "I'll certainly come when I can, but I'm building a fence, you know."

Mrs. Hargrove smiled. "Well, I'll pray you finish it quickly then."

"It might be more than one fence."

Judd stopped before the heavens opened and God struck him dead. He'd already told three lies, and it wasn't even noon. He'd better get to the point. "I was wondering if sometime—it doesn't have to be now—if you'd have a few minutes to talk about raising children? I mean, you seem so good at it."

Mrs. Hargrove chuckled. "You haven't talked to my daughter lately if you think that."

"I didn't know you had a daughter."

Mrs. Hargrove nodded. "I do. A more stubborn, opinionated woman you're not likely to meet than Doris June Hargrove."

"Have I met her?" Judd tried to think of the women of Dry Creek. He couldn't remember any of them who were named Doris.

"She doesn't live around here. She insists on staying up in Anchorage even though her heart is back here where the rest of her belongs. And Charley's son knows she belongs here, too. The two of them are just too stubborn to do anything about it."

"Well, some people take longer to get to know each other."

"Humph," Mrs. Hargrove said. "Those two know each other just fine. Give either one a pencil and paper and they could list every fault of the other in a minute. They'd enjoy doing it, too."

"Well, then, maybe they're happier being apart."

"They're miserable and it's time someone did something about it."

"Well—" Judd started and stopped. He hoped she didn't mean *he* should do anything. He didn't even know either one of them. There hardly seemed anything to say. "Maybe someone will."

Mrs. Hargrove nodded. "That's the first thing you need to learn about being a parent. Sometimes you need to step into your child's business and make it your own."

"Bobby and Amanda are both still a little young for love problems," Judd said. He didn't mention his own problems with the opposite sex. He wasn't sure he'd want Mrs. Hargrove to fix his love life. She looked unstoppable.

"Of course they are. This is information for the future."

"I'm looking more at the next few months," Judd said. "You know, things like nightmares and missing their mother and braids."

"Braids?"

Judd nodded. "I don't know how to braid hair, and Amanda wants her hair to look like Lizette's."

"Oh, of course," Mrs. Hargrove nodded. "It's perfectly obvious that Amanda wants some motherly affection from Lizette."

"It is?"

Mrs. Hargrove nodded. "And it's a good thing. Spending time with Lizette will make her feel better."

"She wants to invite Lizette over for Thanksgiving dinner, but—"

"You're not one of those men who think women are the only ones who should cook, are you?"

Judd shook his head. "I'm not opposed to cooking; I'm just not sure how good I am at it."

"Oh, you'll do fine with cooking a turkey dinner. You just get a bag for the turkey, and I can give you some simple recipes to see you through. You might need to buy a pie though."

"Got a couple in the freezer."

"Well, then, you're all set. I just wish a broken heart was as easy to mend."

Judd looked up in alarm. It was a bit extreme to say his heart was broken. Dented a little maybe, especially after the cool way Lizette was acting toward him today, but not broken. Not at all. "People make too much of broken hearts."

"So you think I shouldn't do anything to make Doris realize she's still in love with Charley's son?" Mrs. Hargrove looked worried.

"Don't listen to me," Judd rushed to say. "I don't know anything about this kind of stuff."

He hadn't even known she was talking about some-one else, that's how much he didn't know.

"I'm sure she'll appreciate whatever you do for her," Judd added.

Mrs. Hargrove chuckled. "I wouldn't go that far, but we'll see. In the meantime, why don't I teach you to braid hair after class today?"

Judd nodded in gratitude just as he heard his name being called from the back room.

"Excuse me," he said to Mrs. Hargrove. "That's Amanda calling."

"Look at your hat," Amanda said with a squeal when Judd entered the back room.

Lizette had found an old sofa for the back room and a mound of colorful costumes were spread out on it. It looked as though some of the accessories were sitting on the square table in one corner as well. There was a curtain at one end of the room, and Judd figured the bed was behind it.

He wondered how anyone could make an old room look so inviting. Then he took a good look at the hat Amanda was pointing at.

"It's real red," Judd said. He figured that was an understatement. Some reds could be dignified. This one wasn't. It was bright enough to light up the darkness. "And it's so big."

The hat was two feet tall.

"Well, you are a nutcracker," Lizette said patiently.

"But I didn't know I was a *giant* nutcracker."

Judd didn't need to look over at Pete to know the

man was snickering. He could hear the cowboy trying to contain his laughter even if he didn't look at him.

"Remember, the Nutcracker fights back," Judd said as he looked over at Pete.

"What? Are you going to slap me with your top hat?" Pete said as he chuckled.

"Oh, no, you can't damage the costumes," Lizette said. "We're going to need to return them when we finish."

"I'll be careful," Judd said. He wouldn't need a hat anyway to fight back against the cowboy.

"And, Pete, you'll be careful too, won't you?" Lizette asked, turning to the cowboy. "Your tail is a little fragile."

Judd started to grin. "His tail?"

Pete stopped laughing. "My tail?"

"Well, you are a mouse," Lizette said.

Amanda and Bobby both giggled. Judd thought he heard Charley give a snort or two as well.

"Rat," Pete corrected. "You said I was a rat."

"Mouse. Rat. They both have tails," Lizette said as she reached into a bag.

Judd grinned even wider. The tail Lizette pulled out of the bag had to be five feet long. And it was pink.

"I can't wear pink," Pete said.

Lizette frowned as she looked at the tail. "It's not exactly pink. It's more puce than anything. Your whole costume is puce."

Judd could see that the costume was pink.

"Maybe I could have my tail chopped off," Pete said. "I bet there are rats that've run into trouble and are missing part of their tail. You know, the fighter kind of rats, like I will be."

"But the tail balances out the ears," Lizette said as she pulled two pink ears out of the bag.

Pete was speechless.

Judd decided his hat wasn't such a bad thing. "If you don't like the look of your ears, maybe you should get a hat."

"Well, at least I have to have something to fight with, don't I?" Pete finally said. "I mean, I have to have something to fight with—like a knife or something."

"You have teeth," Lizette said as she also pulled out a rat's head.

Judd had to admit the head looked like a fighter rat. An uglier mask he'd never seen.

"That's more like it," Pete said as he picked up the mask and turned it around.

"Well, everyone try on their hats and heads. I want to be sure everything fits," Lizette said.

Judd looked around him at all of the other dancers. Mrs. Hargrove had come into the room and was fingering a billowing white dress that must be the Snow Queen outfit. Charley was trying on an old tweed bathrobe that was the costume for the narrator. Judd wished *he'd* been the narrator. The bathrobe looked comfortable. Amanda was, of course, eyeing the Sugar Plum Fairy costume that was over in the corner. Even Bobby and the twins looked happy, since they were going to be either mice or toy soldiers in the first part of the ballet and snowflakes at the end.

Judd realized he'd never been in anything like this in his life. His uncle had thought school itself was a waste of time, so Judd had never tried out for any school plays. There were always chores to do. The closest thing to costumes he'd ever seen were the clown costumes at the rodeo and everyone knew those clowns were not for fun.

Judd decided he liked the thought of playing a part in something like this ballet. Especially now that he'd seen the tail Pete had to wear and realized he wasn't going to be the only man who was wearing a ridiculous costume.

Besides, Judd thought as he saw Amanda and Bobby, he'd never seen the two of them so excited, and it was worth making a fool of himself to see them having such a good time.

Chapter Ten

The first official rehearsal of the Dry Creek Nutcracker ballet was underway. An X was taped to the floor where the artificial tree would be. Charley was sitting on a folding chair next to the fireplace he had built out of cardboard. Mrs. Hargrove was backstage helping the Sugar Plum Fairy adjust her wings. The Curtis twins were being good little mice and sitting in the corner until it was time for them to run across the stage. Bobby was sitting next to the twins in his tin soldier costume. Pete was looking at his new mouse head in the mirror by the practice bars. Judd was holding his hat and frowning at it.

Yes, Lizette thought to herself, they were really going to be able to do this. Even though this was the first time on stage for all of her performers, they already looked like a typical group of ballet students. The only thing that was missing was for one of the performers to be sick.

Lizette had changed into her Clara costume—with Amanda choosing the Sugar Plum Fairy part and no other young girls clamoring for the role, Lizette had decided to adapt it for herself. For the first time today, she felt as if she was the teacher and had everything under control. Generally, Clara had several different costumes during the performance, but Lizette had decided to keep her costume simple. It was a yellow dress with a short skirt. Clara was a young girl, so Lizette had braided her hair into a single braid down her back and tied the end with a big yellow ribbon.

"Let me get the narrator's book and we'll begin," Lizette said.

Madame Aprele said the book she'd sent was a condensed story of the Nutcracker that she had used for one of her own productions years ago when she was first starting her school. She'd eliminated some of the scenes and changed others. She'd promised Lizette that it was a very simple rendition of the classic ballet. Lizette had briefly reviewed the narration and was ready to begin.

"Everyone take your places," Lizette said as she gave Mrs. Hargrove the audiocassette tape to put into the small stereo system Lizette had set up earlier.

* * *

Judd knew ballerinas were supposed to glide, but seeing Lizette dance the first dance left him breathless. She was dipping and bowing and soaring all over the practice floor. And while Lizette was moving, Charley kept reading from the narration about a young girl and her brother who were given special gifts at Christmas time.

The sun was starting to set, and Charley asked Mrs. Hargrove to bring him a lamp that was along the side of the room.

Once the lamp was there, Lizette danced in the circle of light it gave.

Judd was watching Lizette so closely that he didn't notice when his cue came.

"The Nutcracker," Charley cleared his throat and repeated a little louder. "When Clara opened her present, she saw the Nutcracker."

"Just walk into the circle of light," Lizette directed. "You're not alive at this point, so no one will expect you to move."

Judd moved into the circle of light.

"You mean I'm your present?" Judd whispered to Lizette in dismay. "Your Christmas present?"

Judd had gotten Amanda a doll for Christmas with eyes that lit up depending on what kind of eye makeup the girl put on the doll. Judd didn't pretend to know much about little girls, but he was willing to bet that very few of them would be excited about getting a nutcracker for a Christmas present. "Do I at least come with a few walnuts or something?"

"Way to go, Nutcracker," Pete said as he stood by the fireplace holding his rat-king head. "I'd at least bring her some cheese."

"Clara was very excited to open her present and see the Nutcracker," Charley read from the book.

Lizette danced some more, and Judd would swear that the movements of her arms and legs did remind him of an excited little girl. The background music for this part of the ballet was very light and fanciful.

Maybe it wasn't so bad being Lizette's present, Judd thought as he looked over at Pete. The cowboy was still leaning against the wall, only now he was frowning.

"Clara's brother was also given a gift—some toy soldiers," Charley read as Bobby marched forward in a toy soldier costume. "But, even though he liked the toy soldiers, he was jealous of Clara's nutcracker and broke it just when it was time for everyone to go to bed."

Lizette danced into the shadows as the narrator said, "everyone went to bed," leaving the Nutcracker and the toy soldiers in the living room.

"That night after everyone was asleep," Charley kept reading. "Clara and her brother went back downstairs."

"Mice gather over by the fireplace," Lizette whispered, and the Curtis twins hurried over to the fireplace.

"Clara and her brother start playing with the mice," Charley read. Then he reached into the prop bag and pulled out a large wind-up alarm clock. "But then the clock strikes midnight."

Charley pulled a button so the alarm clock would ring.

"When the clock strikes midnight, the mice stop playing. The room becomes darker and is no longer a friendly place. The mice start attacking Clara and her brother. The toy soldiers try to fight back, but they are outnumbered."

The Curtis twins ran up and started flinging their arms around Bobby, who was the toy soldier.

In the middle of the action, Lizette danced around the stage like a wounded bird.

"Seeing that Clara is in trouble, the Nutcracker comes to life and starts to defend her from the mice."

"From the mice?" Judd said. "I thought I was going to fight that Rat King."

Judd figured he shouldn't even have worried. The day he wasn't equal to two little kids was the day he'd give up ballet.

Judd spun around on his tiptoes and pulled the cardboard sword out of the sheath on his belt. Then he tried to dance to the music while he fought back the mice. Of course, he was careful not to fight too hard. He didn't want to discourage the Curtis twins in their mice roles.

"Gradually, it looks like the toy soldiers and the nutcracker are pushing back the mice, and then a giant rat comes bursting out of the fireplace."

Pete crawled out of the front of the fireplace. Of course, the cowboy was on his knees and it took a moment for him to stand. It took another second for him to roar.

Judd took a deep breath so he wouldn't laugh. Pete's tail was twisted around his shoulders, and his ears were as lopsided as a rabbit's.

Pete put his rat head down and charged toward Judd.

"Stop," Lizette commanded. "I have to show you how to stage a fight."

Judd figured it was too late to stage anything. So he moved to the side and let Pete catch him on the shoulder.

Charley kept reading. "The giant rat keeps fighting the Nutcracker until the Nutcracker is weary."

Judd didn't feel the least tired. He rather liked the look of concern he saw on Lizette's face. It might take a charging rat for her to worry about his well-being, but it was nice to know that she could do so with the proper encouragement.

"But we need to stage the action," Lizette said. "There shouldn't be any physical contact."

"How am I going to hit him if I can't touch him?" Pete said as he raised his head.

"You pretend. We all pretend," Lizette said.

"It's okay. He can touch me," Judd said.

Pete lowered his head. "Let the story continue—"

Charley cleared his throat. "The Mouse King gets ready for one final attack. The toy soldier is lying on the floor. Only the Nutcracker is left, and he is wounded."

Pete pawed the floor like a bull would do before it charged.

Judd figured this was the final act for him.

"Clara sees the Mouse King get ready to attack and puts herself between the rat and the Nutcracker," Charley reads.

"What?" Judd said.

"What?" the rat echoed.

"I can fight my own battles," Judd said. He'd thought there was nothing worse than dying in this battle. He was wrong. He'd never live it down if the Nutcracker hid behind a woman's skirts.

"I'd never hit a lady," the rat said.

"You don't have to hit me," Lizette hissed. "Remember, there's no physical contact. Everything is staged."

"B-but, still—" Pete stammered.

"Besides, you don't hit me in the story," Lizette whispered. "I hit you."

Charley turned a page in the book and continued. "Clara takes off one of her shoes and throws it at the Mouse King."

Lizette threw her dance slipper at the rat.

"The shoe hits the Mouse King and topples him," Charley continued.

Pete still stood in astonishment.

"Lie down," the Curtis twins whispered to him. They were both already lying on the floor where they had fallen in battle. "You're dead."

"From a shoe?" Pete asked. "I get beat by a shoe?"

Judd shook his head. He supposed he should be happy that the Mouse King was defeated, but he had to wish right along with Pete that it had happened another way. It didn't do Judd's image any good either to be rescued by a woman and her shoe.

Pete reluctantly slid to the floor. "Even if I'm dead, I'm not closing my eyes."

Charley was fumbling in the bag and the music was starting to soar.

"Because of the bravery of Clara and the Nutcracker, the Nutcracker comes to life and becomes a man," Charley read.

Judd liked the sound of that.

The music soared even further.

"When Clara sees that her beloved Nutcracker is alive, she kisses him," Charley read.

"She what?" Lizette said.

"She does?" Judd grinned.

"Well, nobody told *me* that," the Mouse King said, and it looked like he was going to rise again.

Charley looked up. "That's what it says right here."

"Madame Aprele must have changed the text," Lizette said as she walked over to Charley and looked at the book for herself.

"I think a kiss would be nice," Mrs. Hargrove said from the sidelines. "Everybody likes a little romance in a ballet."

"Well, I guess it could be a stage kiss," Lizette said as she walked back to Judd.

"And you need to take his hat off for when he turns into a prince," Charley whispered. "Those are the directions."

Judd forgot all about the room that was around them. He forgot about the dead mice lying on the floor and the live rat looking ready to pounce. He forgot about the Sugar Plum Fairy sitting on the sidelines watching him. All Judd could think about was the green eyes staring straight at him.

Why, she's nervous, Judd thought to himself. The woman who had been treating him all morning like he was a raw recruit and she was the drill sergeant was actually nervous to be this close to him.

"It'll be okay," he said softly.

"It's just a stage kiss," Lizette reminded him.

Judd wasn't even going to ask what a stage kiss was. He figured a raw recruit should be able to plead ignorance.

Judd took the tall hat off his head and set it on the floor beside them. He'd never yet kissed a woman with his hat still on his head, and he wasn't going to start now.

The background music dipped, and the green in Lizette's eyes deepened. She must have guessed his intent, because she gave a soft gasp and her mouth formed a perfect O.

Judd kissed her. He'd meant to satisfy his curiosity with the kiss. He'd been wanting to kiss Lizette since he saw her hanging that sign in her window. When he kissed her, though, he forgot all about the reasons he wanted to kiss her. He just needed to kiss her. That was all there was to it.

Judd finally heard Charley clearing his throat. Judd wasn't sure how long the man had been sitting there doing that, but he figured it must have been for some time. The others were looking at them in astonishment.

Somehow Judd's arms had gotten around Lizette and she was nestled in the curve of his shoulder. She still had her face turned into him, and Judd felt protective of her.

"We were just doing this stage kiss," Judd finally managed to say. His voice sounded a little hoarse, but he was at least able to get the words out.

"Uh-huh," Pete said from where he lay by the fireplace. "You mean the one where there's no actual contact?"

"It's the one the movie stars do," Judd said as he felt Lizette move away from his shoulder a little.

"Sometimes," Lizette said as she took a steadying breath, "actors get very involved in their roles and forget who they really are."

"I'm not getting that involved in being a rat," Pete said as he stood up.

Judd had to admit he wasn't asking himself how a Nutcracker would feel about anything, either. He had enough trouble just knowing how Judd Bowman felt.

Lizette stepped out of his arms and Judd let her go. In that instant, he knew exactly how Judd Bowman felt. He felt as though a truck had run him over, and he wanted to beg it to come back and run him over again. He couldn't breathe.

"I think we've gone far enough in the story for today," Lizette said as she stepped even farther away from Judd. "We'll meet again tomorrow—"

Charley cleared his throat. "But tomorrow is Thanksgiving."

"Oh, yes." Lizette blushed. "I mean on Friday. We'll meet to practice on Friday. And I hope all of you have a nice Thanksgiving."

Judd was starting to breathe normally again.

"But we were going to ask you," Amanda whispered as she came up beside Judd and put her hand in his.

Judd let his fingers curl around the little hand.

"We *were* going to ask her, weren't we?" Amanda asked as she looked up at Judd.

"Yes, pumpkin," Judd said as he tried to get himself to focus. He felt as though he'd been bucked off a stallion and hit his back hard coming down. He looked down to see what Amanda wanted.

But Amanda was no longer there. She'd slipped her hand out of his and gone over to Lizette.

"We want you to come eat Thanksgiving with us," Amanda said loud and clear. "And I'm going to help make the potatoes. Cousin Judd said I could. Bobby gets to help with the vegetables."

"Oh, that's very sweet," Lizette said as she looked over at Judd with a question in her eyes. "But I'm sure you'll be—"

Judd could see the excitement start to dim in Amanda's eyes. If he'd had his wits about him, he'd have given her some excuse about why they couldn't invite Lizette. He knew it did a man like him no good to start dreaming about a woman like Lizette. He could never give her all that she deserved. But he couldn't put his comfort ahead of Amanda's happiness, either.

"Please come," he finally said.

"We're going to have dinner and then go to the candle service at church. Bobby and I get to take the candles we made up front. Cousin Judd said we could," Amanda added.

"I'm sure you both have beautiful candles," Lizette said as she put her hand on Amanda's shoulder.

"I made one for you, too," Amanda said softly.

"Oh," Lizette said, and then she looked at Judd.

Judd figured that was when she decided. He noticed she lifted her chin a little for courage.

"I'd love to join you for dinner," Lizette finally said. "And church, too."

Judd hadn't realized he was holding his breath again until he let it out. So, they were having company for Thanksgiving dinner after all. And then they'd all be going to church.

"I'm doing vegetables," Bobby said as he stood up from the floor. "Mrs. Hargrove told me how."

"Green beans in mushroom soup topped with fried onion rings," Mrs. Hargrove said from the sidelines. "It's the simplest vegetable recipe I know, and it's good."

"I could bring something," Lizette offered.

Judd noticed the color was coming back to her cheeks.

"I think we have everything we need," he said.

"You're sure? I could make a pie," Lizette said.

"You can?" Charley said as he stood up from his narrator chair. "What kind of pies can you make?"

"Well, most kinds," Lizette said.

"If that don't beat everything," Charley said to no one in particular. "She can make pies."

"I like apple," Bobby said. "Can you make apple?"

Lizette smiled. "I'll need to run over to Miles City to get some apples, but I need to go later today anyway to get some flyers printed for the Nutcracker. I want to post them around."

"You use real apples?" Charley asked. "It's not that canned filling?"

"Oh, no," Lizette said. "There's nothing like real apple pie."

"Hallelujah," Charley said.

"I could make one for you while I'm making pies," Lizette offered.

Charley nodded and sighed. "I'd sure be happy if you did."

Judd figured Lizette had already made him happy even if she never made a pie.

"I've heard an apple pie is the way to a man's heart," Mrs. Hargrove said softly as she stood next to Judd.

Judd remembered Mrs. Hargrove was in a match-making mood. He wasn't so sure he wanted the whole countryside to know his heart was taken by Lizette. When the word got out about the pies, Judd figured he'd be one of a long line of broken-hearted men hoping for a kind word from the ballet teacher.

"Lemon's more my pie," Judd said.

"Oh," Mrs. Hargrove said in surprise. "I meant Bobby's heart."

Judd smiled. "Of course."

Judd wondered how he'd made it to adulthood without understanding women.

"Although, now that you mention it," Mrs. Hargrove said thoughtfully. She smiled at Judd. "That was a very unusual stage kiss."

"I'm new to the stage stuff."

Mrs. Hargrove smiled. "You're learning fast."

Judd nodded. He was a marked man and Mrs. Hargrove knew it. His only consolation was that the older woman seemed to be kind. He hoped that she also knew how to keep a secret. Judd wasn't sure he could stand for the state of his heart to become a topic of common gossip around Dry Creek.

Chapter Eleven

Lizette put the lemon pie on the table. She could as well have laid a snake down in front of the man.

"But you made apple pie," Judd said.

They'd already finished their dinner of roasted turkey and mashed potatoes and green been casserole, and it was time to have pie. Lizette had kept the lemon pie in a box in the refrigerator while they ate because it needed to stay cool. She hadn't realized until now that Judd must have thought it was another apple pie in the box.

Lizette had made two apple pies for Bobby. She'd delivered the extra pie wrapped in tin foil so he could freeze it for a later meal. She'd also made an apple pie for Charley. Charley and Bobby had been delighted with their pies. Judd, however, looked horrified.

"You said you liked lemon pie," Lizette reminded

him. She tried to keep her voice calm. He was looking at her with questions in his eyes. What could she say? She'd made the man the pie because, well, "I had left-over crust."

There. That should satisfy him that she wasn't attempting to lure him into a relationship. The pie was simply a pie.

Lizette took a knife like the one she'd used to cut the apple pie and cut several small pieces of the lemon pie. "I made three pies with the crust I had, and there wasn't enough dough left to make another apple pie because it takes double the amount of crust, so I made a single-crust pie. Lemon."

"Oh." Judd seemed relieved even though he didn't put his plate forward for more pie like the kids were doing. "I wouldn't want you to go to any extra trouble. I mean, I like apple pie, too."

"Besides, it's really for everyone," Lizette continued. She used a pie lifter to put a piece of pie on Bobby's outstretched plate and then on Amanda's plate. "I'm sure the kids like lemon meringue pie."

Amanda nodded from her side of the table. "And chocolate. We like chocolate pie, too, with the white stuff."

"Maybe next time, sweetie," Lizette said as she put the pie lifter on the plate next to the lemon pie.

Amanda swallowed. "But what if my mother comes back before you make the pie?"

"I'm sure she'll wait long enough for you to eat a piece of pie," Lizette said, making a mental note to get the ingredients for a chocolate pie the next time she drove into Miles City. It wouldn't hurt to make a crust and keep it in the freezer so she could whip up a pie at a moment's notice.

Actually, while she was making crusts, maybe she should make several crusts. The people of Dry Creek seemed to like their pies. Well, except for Judd, of course. He was still just looking at the lemon pie.

Amanda nodded as she took up her fork. "My mom likes pies, too. She always made us a chocolate pie for Christmas."

Lizette watched as Amanda set her fork back down without taking another bite. The girl's lower lip was beginning to tremble.

"What if my mom doesn't get back in time for Christmas?" Amanda asked.

"Oh, sweetie." Lizette pushed her chair back from the table and stood up so she could go around to Amanda and give her a hug. Judd was already there by the time Amanda reached the little girl's chair.

And that was the way it was supposed to be, Lizette told herself as she stood and watched Amanda reach up to go into Judd's arms. Lizette supposed it was the kitchen table that had confused her. The table was square and had a place for each of them—Judd,

Amanda, Bobby, and herself, Lizette. The table had made her feel like she was part of their family.

But Judd was the one the children turned to for comfort. He was the one who was standing in for their mother.

"Don't worry," Judd said softly to Amanda as he held her close. "I've already asked the sheriff to look for your mother, and he said he'll do everything he can to track her down."

"Maybe she's hiding from our dad," Bobby said from his place at the table. "Maybe she doesn't know he's in jail."

"Maybe," Judd agreed.

Lizette admired the way Judd was so honest with the children. He didn't pretend that they were asking questions they had no right to ask. He didn't gloss over the fact that their father was in jail and that their mother hadn't returned when she'd said she would. He didn't promise them things that he couldn't deliver, either.

As a child, Lizette remembered her mother always being so cheerful about their difficulties that she had never really told Lizette what was going on. Lizette had never even known what disease her father had died of until just before her mother was diagnosed with cancer. Lizette had wondered if her mother finally realized all of the things she hadn't told Lizette over the years and was trying to make up for it by telling her everything she could before she died. Lizette wished her mother had started really talking to her years before she did.

"You must miss your mother very much," Lizette said.

Amanda nodded, her head against Judd's shoulder. "She's not going to be here for her candle."

"Amanda made her a candle," Bobby said quietly from where he still sat at the table. "I told her there was no need to make one. Mom won't be home in time to light it in church tonight."

"We can light it for her," Judd said.

"But she won't be able to say what she's thankful for—" Amanda lifted her head away from Judd's shoulder and protested. "You have to say what you're thankful for when you light the candle. That's what Mrs. Hargrove says."

"I know what your mother's thankful for," Judd said. "The two of you."

"Will you say the words?" Bobby asked. "Amanda and me want to light the candle, but we want someone else to say the words."

Judd nodded. "I'll be happy to say them for your mother."

Amanda had stopped crying by now. "Do you think she'll be able to hear when we say the words? No matter where she is?"

Lizette held her breath. She wondered if Judd would lie to the children.

Judd thought for a minute. "If she doesn't hear them, I'm going to remember them so I can tell her what they were when she gets here."

Amanda nodded. "I'm going to remember them, too."

Lizette vowed she would remember them as well, even though it was absolutely unnecessary. She knew she wouldn't have much of a chance to talk with the children's mother when she came back into town, and if Lizette did get a chance to talk to her, Lizette thought she'd probably have something else to discuss with the woman.

For starters, Lizette knew she'd like to ask Judd's cousin how she could have left her two children for such a long time. Didn't she know they would worry? Lizette knew if *she* was lucky enough to have children like the ones in front of her now, *she* wouldn't be able to leave them with someone else.

"This pie's real good," Bobby said. He'd taken a bite of the lemon pie.

Amanda squirmed to be let down from Judd's arms, and he settled her back in her chair.

"Let me taste it," Amanda said as she took her own bite of the lemon pie.

Lizette couldn't believe that was it. One minute the

children had been in tears, and the next they were smiling because of pie. Even Judd was looking happier than he had a few minutes ago.

"Lemon pie has always been my favorite," Judd said as he helped himself to a piece of the pie. "Maybe that's what I'm going to say I'm thankful for tonight in church. Lemon pie."

Amanda giggled. "You can't be thankful for pie. You have to be thankful for people. Mrs. Hargrove says that's the most important thing."

Lizette felt a sudden dart of alarm. People? She was supposed to be thankful for people? "Can't we be thankful for other things, too?"

Amanda thought for a moment and then nodded. "But they have to be big things."

"And you can't be thankful for dragons," Bobby added. "The Curtis twins told me that. One year they told everyone they were thankful for dragons, and everyone said they were cute. Some of the women even pinched their cheeks. I don't want to get my cheeks pinched."

"I could be thankful for my dog," Judd said. "He's turned out to be a fine watchdog for a stray."

Amanda nodded. "A dog would be a good thankful."

Lizette wondered if she could be thankful for a whole town. She was beginning to feel like she had a home among the people of Dry Creek, even though she hadn't expected to feel that way when she moved here.

"I don't know," Judd said as he helped himself to another small piece of lemon pie. "This is awfully good pie. Maybe I could be thankful for the pie *and* my new dog."

Judd smiled at Lizette before she started to eat the piece of pie on her plate. "I haven't even said a proper thank-you yet for the pie. It's excellent. I don't think I've ever had such good lemon pie."

"Lemon pie's not that hard to make," Lizette said. "You just have to use real lemons."

"Any pie is hard to make in my opinion," Judd said. "I'm not much of a cook."

"I wouldn't say that. The meal today was wonderful."

When Lizette had arrived, Judd had a dish towel wrapped around his waist and he was mashing potatoes with an old-fashioned masher he said he'd found in the pantry. There had been things left in the house, he explained, from when the Jenkins family lived here.

Lizette figured that the curtains had been one of the things left in the house by Mrs. Jenkins. They had to have been hung over the sink by a woman. They were white threadbare cotton, and they had tiny embroidered pansies on the bottom of them. The pansies were lavender, pink and yellow.

The kitchen was a comfortable room that had seen its share of family meals over the years. Lizette had noticed that the doorway from the kitchen to the living room had a series of old cuts in the side of it and two new cuts. The wood of the old cuts was gray, but the color of the newer cuts was golden.

Judd had noticed her looking at the cuts. "Kids' growing marks. I thought I should add Amanda and Bobby. It took me long enough to figure out what the other cuts were there for—I figured some fancy exercise machine or maybe someone just standing there who had a new knife and wanted to try it out. But the marks were too deliberate for either of those."

Lizette had smiled. She knew enough about Judd's childhood to understand how bewildering it must have seemed to mark a child's growth. It was a homey thing that spoke of love and attention.

Lizette wondered if she could list as her grateful the fact that she was a guest in this house today for Thanksgiving dinner. She had expected to have a cup of canned soup in her studio. Of course, some of the other families in Dry Creek had invited her home with them for Thanksgiving dinner. She'd refused all of the other invitations. She didn't want to be with a family that was whole. In a family like that she would be extra. But in this little makeshift family she felt like she had a place, even if it was only for the day.

"I have lots of eggs," Judd said. He'd finished his piece of pie, and he pushed the plate away from him.

"If you want any eggs for your baking, just let me know. You're welcome to all you need. I got some chickens after the kids came, so we have lots of eggs."

"Thanks. That's helpful." Lizette figured it was the Montana way to give small gifts like that to your neighbors. "And if you want any baked goods, let me know. Doughnuts. Pies. Anything."

Lizette figured that would be the best gift she could give any of the men around here. After she'd agreed to make doughnuts for the one cowboy, she'd gotten five more orders for closer to Christmastime. It was apparently going to be a merry Christmas in the bunkhouses around here.

"You don't need to pay me with baked goods," Judd said as he stood up from the table. "You're still welcome to the eggs."

"Well, I have to do something for you," Lizette said as she stood up, too. "You've invited me to dinner and offered me eggs and—"

Judd walked over to the kitchen sink. "If you're set on paying me back, you can help with the dishes. I'll wash if you dry."

"Yes, but doing dishes isn't enough."

"You haven't seen how many dishes we have," Judd said as he turned the faucet on and let the water start to run in the sink. "And I'm including the pots and pans."

In the end, Lizette didn't dry many of the dishes.

Bobby and Amanda both wanted to help dry dishes, so Lizette found her job involved more reaching the tall shelves to put the dishes away and handing clean towels to the two children and scratching Judd's back.

"Maybe you should see a doctor," Lizette said the second time Judd asked her to scratch between his shoulder blades. "Maybe you have a rash."

"That's the place," Judd said with a sigh as her fingers gave a gentle scratch to the area next to his right shoulder blade.

Lizette let her fingers settle into the lazy circles the man seemed to like. "Maybe there's some cream that would stop the itch."

"No, it'll be fine," Judd said lazily, and then seemed to remember something. "Not that it's a rash. I'm a perfectly healthy specimen. No rashes. No long-term medical problems at all. Good teeth."

"He's got a funny toe," Amanda whispered as she leaned over to Lizette. "Have him show you his funny toe."

Judd figured he might as well give up and declare himself a freak of nature. He sure didn't know much about how to make a woman want to date him. Not that there was much chance that Lizette would want to date a man like him anyway, even if his health was reasonably good. No, she'd go for someone ten years younger, someone more her age. Someone about the age of Pete.

"I think Pete has a rash though," Judd offered. "Nothing serious. Something to do with the cattle."

"It's not mad cow disease, is it?"

Judd groaned. He wanted to scare Lizette away from Pete, not away from the whole town of Dry Creek. "No, I think it was just a little poison ivy he got in one of the cattle pastures on the Elkton ranch."

It was this past summer when Pete had stepped into some poison ivy, but Judd didn't think he needed to be that specific. The hardware store had been buzzing with the news the whole week last summer. Apparently poison ivy was rare in these parts of Montana. But, for all Judd knew, the cowboy still had the occasional itch from the experience.

"I don't have any poison ivy on my place," Judd added just to be on the safe side. "No rashes. No poison ivy. No mad cow disease."

"Yes, but—" Lizette stopped scratching and leaned sideways so she could smile at him. "You do have that funny toe."

Judd didn't know what had possessed him to try to tell the kids the story of the little piggies. He'd seen a woman in a supermarket once playing the game with her baby's toes while they sat on a bench beside the bakery. Judd had been so taken with the singsong way the woman had recited the nursery rhyme that he'd stayed and listened to her for half an hour.

When the kids were so scared that first night they were at his place, Judd had remembered that nursery rhyme. It was the only thing he knew to do to quiet little kids, and Amanda made him tell the rhyme again and again even after she stopped being afraid. Unfortunately, she wanted to use his toes to represent the little piggies, and not her own.

"Amanda thinks my little toe is too big," Judd finally admitted.

Amanda nodded emphatically. "It's not the little-piggy toe at all. It's supposed to go wee-wee all the way home and it's not wee at all."

Lizette smiled. "So it's not broken or anything?"

"Nope, just too big," Judd said.

Lizette smiled at him again, and suddenly Judd felt ten years younger. Maybe he could hope, after all. Maybe she hadn't noticed he was that much older than she was. Maybe she didn't care if he had a big little toe. Maybe she wouldn't even care that he didn't know much about family life and was a poor prospect as a husband and an even poorer prospect as a father.

Maybe—Judd stopped himself. He would have been safer thinking that he could turn his little toe into a squealing pig than that he could turn himself into someone worthy of Lizette.

Judd brought his dreams to a complete halt. He didn't know much about family life, but he had learned a few things from the kids while they'd been staying with him, and one thing he did know—it didn't pay for a man to have dreams that outreached any realistic hope he had of grabbing hold of those dreams. He'd miss the kids when their mother came back, but he could live with that pain.

What he couldn't live with was getting himself to thinking he could make a home of his own with Lizette. When that dream came crashing down, he'd feel the pain for the rest of his life.

No, it was better to stop the dreaming in the first place.

Chapter Twelve

The steps to the church didn't look as hard to climb at night as they had been on Sunday morning. Maybe it was because Lizette knew there were friendly faces inside. At least she knew what was going to happen this time when she went through those double doors at the top of the stairs.

The kids had given her and Judd complete details on what to expect. They'd mentioned that everyone sat in the pews and different people went up to set their very own candle on the table next to the pulpit. Then the person would light their candle and tell everyone what he or she was thankful for during the past year. Then the person went back to their pew and sat down.

Essentially, Lizette told herself, it was up, candle, thanks and down. She could handle that even in unfamiliar territory like a church.

Lizette had to admit to herself, however, that she no longer felt as much like a stranger as she had expected. The people from the church weren't as critical of her as she had imagined they would be. No one seemed to care if she wore a hat when no one else did or if she had to read the words to the hymns from the songbook when everyone else knew the words by heart.

So, she told herself, she should relax. Besides, tonight there wouldn't be any lessons on how people should treat each other, so there would be nothing that could cause her any awkward tears. She didn't want to risk ending up on Judd's shoulder again. Not after that kiss.

That kiss had been superb acting. She had felt the Nutcracker's passion all the way down to her toes. But it was the mistake of a novice to imagine that the person acting a role next to you onstage actually meant those feelings for you. That's what made a play a play. It was pretend. Lizette thought of all of the actors who had played Romeo and Juliet over the years. Did they get married to each other after the play? No. What happened on stage was pretend.

Lizette must have given herself that speech a dozen times over the last few days, yet she still felt the need to remind herself.

Apart from that kiss, Judd had given absolutely no indication that he was interested in her in any way except as a dinner guest and ballet instructor. In fact, usually he just frowned at her. She didn't know why she was having these fluttery feelings about him, but it had to stop. She didn't want to embarrass herself by making him worry that she was getting romantic ideas just because he'd thrown himself into the part of the Nutcracker with enthusiasm.

And the kiss—well—what man wouldn't be pleased to know he was a prince instead of a wooden kitchen utensil used to break apart nut shells? Didn't she remember that football players kissed their teammates after winning a particularly important game? Of course, she didn't think they kissed them on the lips, but that was only a matter of location. The principle of the victory kiss was the same.

No, she had no reason to take Judd's kiss personally. She was a professional. She knew how people threw themselves into acting.

Lizette looked over at Judd. They were standing at the bottom of the church stairs as they had before, only this time it was dark and it was hard to read any expression on Judd's face. She did notice that he wasn't frowning though, and that was a good sign with Judd. Now that she thought about it, she didn't think he'd frowned at all today. Except, of course, when he'd first seen the lemon pie she'd made for him.

"You've got your candle?" Judd turned to Lizette and asked.

Lizette nodded. Amanda had already given her the candle she had made for her to use tonight. It was a short pink candle, and Amanda had put glittery sequins all over it, because, she said, it reminded her of the ballet costumes.

"I've got mine, too," Amanda said as she held out her blue candle. She had decorated it with the same kind of sequins and sparkles that she'd used on Lizette's.

"Mine are here," Judd said as he patted the pocket of his coat.

Lizette had already seen the two candles he carried. One was the candle the kids had made for him and the other was the one they had made for their mother.

Lizette had smiled when she had seen the candle the kids had made for Judd. They obviously couldn't agree on what kind of candle Judd would like, so the candle had been dipped in red coloring on one side and green coloring on the other. The two colors mixed in places and made long rivulets of dark purple. The one thing the kids had seemed to agree on was cow stickers, and they had put them all over the candle. The candle they had made for their mother was a tall yellow taper with stickers of two long-stemmed white roses on the side of it.

Bobby hadn't shown any of them his candle. "It's green," was all he would say.

Judd and Lizette seemed to take a deep breath at the

same time and they looked over at each other and nodded. Then they each took the hand of a child and started to walk up the steps to the church.

The church was transformed at night. Last Sunday morning the light shining into the sanctuary from the windows had made the place look homey. The light had also clearly shown up the nicks in the back of the pews and the scuff marks on the floor by the entry.

But tonight, there were no nicks or marks showing. There were light sconces on the side walls and a dim glow came from each one. There was also an overhead light that gave a muted light. Instead of the imperfections of the room, the yellow light made everything look richer.

Lizette glanced over at Judd. It also made everyone look more handsome.

"Do they have a ballet here, too?" Amanda whispered in a hushed tone as they stood at the back of the church.

"No, sweetie, those are choir robes," Lizette answered as she followed the direction of Amanda's gaze.

Two women were standing near the piano and they had on long robes made of midnight-blue satin with white collars. They were leaning over to read some music that the pianist was playing. From where they stood, Lizette could hear the soft hum of the women's voices as they sang a song.

"Oh, welcome," Mrs. Hargrove said as she and Charley walked down the aisle toward them. "I'm so glad you came."

"We wouldn't miss it," Judd said as he shook the hand Charley offered. "We have some special candles to light. Besides, I wanted to talk with the sheriff if he's here."

Judd still hadn't talked with the sheriff, and he wanted to know a little more about when the kids' father was coming up for trial. Not that Judd expected to go to the trial. He just thought he should know unless anyone said anything in front of the kids.

"Sheriff Wall had some kind of business that took him out of town," Charley said. "Asked me and my son to give the Billings police a call if anything went wrong around here."

"Does he usually leave someone in charge when he's gone?" Judd hadn't realized how much he'd counted on calling the sheriff if trouble did come up with Amanda and Bobby's father.

"There was never any need for him to leave someone in charge," Charley said. "I think he's just worried because—" Charley glanced at the children and lowered his voice until only Judd could hear "—well, we don't usually have something in town that a criminal wants that much. But now—well, the sheriff said he'd feel easier about leaving the two of us to keep an eye on things, especially until they got the man transferred over to the Billings jail. My son doesn't get into town much except for church, but I'll be around to keep a lookout."

Judd frowned. "Is there a delay with sending him to Billings?"

Charley shrugged. "They needed to wait for an opening. The jail in Billings is full at the moment. So they're keeping him in Miles City."

"There's nothing wrong with the jail in Miles City, is there?"

Charley chuckled. "Nothing some extra heat wouldn't cure. The county doesn't like us to keep folks there in the winter because we can't afford to heat it the way it should be. It tends to be on the cold side."

"But it's secure?" Judd asked.

Charley nodded. "It might not be comfortable, but it's built like a fort."

Judd nodded. He supposed there was no need to worry. The Miles City jail should hold the man, and that was all he cared about.

Mrs. Hargrove smiled down at the children. "Why, look—you've both got your candles."

Judd prepared himself for Amanda to press her face into his leg from shyness, and he had his hand halfway down to reassure her when he realized there was no need. Amanda didn't even look back to see that he was there. She just smiled up at Mrs. Hargrove and started walking down the aisle between the pews.

"We want to get a good pew," Amanda turned around and said to Judd and Lizette.

Judd wondered what made a pew a good pew, but it looked as though Amanda had definite opinions on the matter. If she didn't, Bobby had almost reached her and would no doubt add his advice, as well.

Apparently, going to this church had done something besides make Judd uncomfortable. It had made the children confident in Dry Creek without him.

"I guess they don't need us," Judd said to Lizette now that both children were ahead of them.

Judd looked down to smile at Lizette and was glad he had gotten the words out of his mouth before he did. He'd never seen Lizette in soft light before. He'd seen her in the bright daylight of the ballet studio and the ordinary light of his dinner table. He'd even seen her just minutes ago in the darkness outside as they walked up to the church. But he'd never seen her in soft muted lighting like this.

She was beautiful. Softly beautiful. Stirringly beautiful. She was—

"Whoeee." Pete's voice broke Judd's concentration before he even knew the cowboy had walked up behind them. Not that the cowboy was paying Judd any attention. The man was looking at Lizette like she'd stepped off the pages of a magazine ad for a tropical paradise. "Aren't you something?"

Lizette smiled at the man.

Judd resisted the urge to growl like a guard dog. Well, he tried to resist the urge. No one noticed he didn't quite succeed except for Mrs. Hargrove.

"If you need an antacid, let me know," the older woman said as she looked at him and patted her purse. "I carry a small pharmacy in here. After a big turkey dinner like today, you won't be the only one who needs help digesting it all."

"Thanks, but I'm fine."

Judd told himself he was fine. He was certainly just as fine as Pete.

And Lizette must realize it. She was looking at him now instead of at Pete.

"Maybe Mrs. Hargrove has something in her purse for that rash of yours," Lizette said with a sympathetic tone in her voice.

Judd grimaced. "I don't have a rash." He looked over at Mrs. Hargrove and then at Pete. Their eyes were all bright with curiosity. "I just asked her to scratch my back while I was washing dishes. I just had a little itch. That's all. No rash."

"Hmm," Mrs. Hargrove said with a smile. "Well, I don't think I have anything to treat that with."

"I think I feel an itch working its way up my back

right now," Pete said as he stepped closer to Lizette. "Maybe you could scratch it for me?"

"We've got candles to light," Judd said as he took Lizette's arm and steered her down the aisle.

"Here we are," Amanda whispered from the pew she and Bobby had chosen.

Judd almost groaned again. The two of them had chosen the half pew that was off to the right side of the piano. He figured the pew could hold two adults comfortably. But when you added the two children, they would all be very tight.

The kids were geniuses, Judd told himself ten minutes later. The only way he and Lizette could fit in the pew with the children was if he held Amanda on his lap and Bobby sat next to the piano. That meant he and Lizette were in the middle and pressed close together. It was perfect. Judd could watch the light dance around in Lizette's dark hair as she moved her head, and he was also close enough to smell the faint lilac perfume that she wore.

He was a happy man.

"Can I go up with my candle now?" Amanda asked as she squirmed down off of Judd's lap.

Judd looked around. Several people had taken their candles up, but it didn't look like anyone was standing up right this minute. "Sure. Do you want me to come with you?"

Amanda shook her head. "I can do it."

Judd had to blink his eyes when he saw Amanda walk up in front of the whole congregation and put her candle on the table. A few weeks ago she wouldn't even speak to him, and now she was telling everyone why she was grateful.

"I'm glad I get to be the Sugar Plum Fairy," Amanda said after she put her candle on the table. Then she skipped back to the pew where the rest of them sat.

"You did real good, sweetie," Lizette said to the girl as Amanda crawled back up on Judd's lap.

"You sure did," Judd added. It was Lizette who had worked the change in Amanda. Judd had known how to protect the child, but he hadn't known how to make her so excited about something that she needed to talk about it.

Several more people got up to take their candles to the front of the church. Pete was one of them. He had a plain white candle stuck in the bottom of a tin cup, and he said he was thankful he'd gotten to have Thanksgiving dinner with his mother up by Havre.

"Ah, isn't that sweet?" Lizette murmured.

Judd grunted. He'd been unaware that Pete had a mother.

"And I got to bring her a geranium plant that was blooming," Pete continued. The cowboy held his hat in his hands, and Judd couldn't tell if the other man was sincere or just saying what the women wanted to hear. "She appreciated the plant now because her arthritis is bad and she can't be out much."

"Ah," Lizette sighed. "He's good to visit his mother."

Judd didn't point out that for all they knew the cowboy only ever spent one holiday with her. One holiday didn't mean he visited his mother regularly.

Judd was frowning by the time Pete sat down in his pew. Judd knew he was being uncharitable and it made him irritable. The truth was, Pete probably did know more about family life than *he* did.

Mrs. Hargrove stood up next. The older woman carried a candelabra with several candles in it. She said she was lighting candles for those in her family who couldn't be here. "And one of them should be," she added. "And will be by next Thanksgiving if I have anything to say about it."

"Amen," Charley said from his place in the church, and several people nodded.

Judd noticed that the middle-aged man who sat next to Charley didn't nod like everyone else in the church did. He didn't even smile or look the least bit thankful. That must be Charley's son. Judd wondered if the poor man had any idea what his father and Mrs. Hargrove were planning for him. Probably not. But the man looked like someone who could take care of himself, and Judd had enough of his own trouble to worry about.

Bobby went up with his candle after the Curtis twins had finished.

"I'm thankful that my Mom is okay even if I don't know where she is," Bobby said bravely after he added his candle to the table. Judd noticed Bobby had wrapped a yellow ribbon around the candle. It must have been the ribbon his mother accidentally left when she left the children with Judd.

"Shall we go up now?" Judd whispered in Lizette's ear.

Lizette nodded and stood up when he did.

Judd set Amanda down on the floor so she could walk with them.

Sometimes a man had more to be grateful for than he could share with other people. Having Lizette come up front with him and the kids beside him made him feel humble and proud all at the same time. When they were together in church, Judd felt like he belonged somewhere and to someone. He wondered if church did that to other people.

"I'm grateful that the town gave me a place to set up my ballet studio," Lizette said as she set her pink candle on the table. "It's made my mother's dream come true. I wish she were here to see it."

Judd wished he'd had a chance to meet Lizette's mother. She must have been a special woman to raise someone like Lizette all by herself.

"I have two candles," Judd said as he reached into his pockets. Both Amanda and Bobby were on his right, so he handled their mother's candle to them. "The first candle is for Barbara, Amanda and Bobby's mother. If she were here today, I think she'd tell you that the thing she is most grateful for is her two wonderful children."

Bobby and Amanda carefully set their mother's candle on the table.

Judd pulled the other candle out of his pocket and set it on the table. "As for me, I'm grateful for—" Judd stopped. He meant to say he was grateful for the dog that had wandered onto his farm last spring. And he *was* thankful for the dog. He'd never had a pet before. But he suddenly wanted to be more honest with the people of Dry Creek who were watching him. So he cleared his throat and began again. "I'm most grateful for feeling like I'm part of a family today."

There, Judd told himself. He'd been open and vulnerable and no one had stood up and called him a liar or anything. In fact, what he could see in the dim lighting was that most people were nodding their heads like he was right to be grateful for that. Judd stood with the kids while they waited for Lizette to light her candle.

The rest of the people in the Dry Creek church lit candles. Some of them mentioned being thankful for good health. One or two were thankful for the year's good crops. Still others were grateful that family members were all able to be together for the holiday.

When everyone had finished taking their candles up to the front of the church, the two women in choir robes sang a song about amazing grace. Judd figured they had that about right. He'd never seen much kindness or grace in his life, but he was beginning to think that the people in this church knew something about grace that he didn't. Maybe he should take the kids to church here until their mother came to get them. He'd like for them to know about this amazing grace that was in the song.

He sighed. He guessed if he was going to do this church business, he should do it right. Maybe he could order a tie from the catalog. While he was at it, he'd order a suit, as well.

Judd looked over at Lizette. He wondered if she'd wear that cute little hat to church again if he wore a tie. At least as long as the kids were with him, Judd was pretty sure she'd sit with them in church.

And Sunday was only a couple of days away. Maybe it wouldn't be such a hardship to go to church after all.

Chapter Thirteen

It was the Monday morning after Thanksgiving, and Lizette was making progress on plans for the Nutcracker. She'd seen Mr. Elkton in church yesterday and he'd offered her the use of the barn he owned on the outskirts of Dry Creek for the performance itself. She'd been assured by Mrs. Hargrove that enough people would come to see the Nutcracker performance that they would need to have more space than Lizette had in her dance school.

"Plus, we can set a refreshment table up at one end of the barn for those lovely pastries you mentioned, and we'll need some punch, of course," Mrs. Hargrove said. "Don't you worry about it being a barn. The building hasn't been used as a barn for ten years or more. We keep it clean just for events like this. We'll have our Christmas pageant there on Christmas Eve, so we'll just get things ready earlier and have the Nutcracker in the barn, too."

Lizette planned to have the ballet this coming Friday evening, December 3. She'd walked over to the barn after church yesterday and checked to see if the floor was smooth enough for ballet movements. It was.

Plus, the barn was charming. There were several windows on each side of the barn, and the sunlight showed off the square features of the structure. There were rafters and square trim around the windows and the large double door. The wood was all golden as if it had been polished.

It was easy to believe that there had been other performances in the building. There was even a small sound system that had been wired around the rafters so that the music she used for the Nutcracker would be easier to hear.

"We're getting to be a regular cultural center here in Dry Creek," Mrs. Hargrove continued. "What with the ballet and then the Christmas pageant. I can take my Christmas tree over to the barn anytime you want and Charley can move the fireplace he made over so we'll be all set for the ballet. And with the hayloft, there's even stairs you can use for when Clara goes up to her bedroom to sleep." Mrs. Hargrove stopped all of a sudden and shook her head. "There I go again. Making everyone's plans for them. I'm working on controlling my organizing spirit this Christmas."

"Don't worry about it with me," Lizette said. "I'm happy to have a little guidance."

Mrs. Hargrove nodded. "Well, I suppose you do need someone to show you the ropes for the first time. It'd be a pity if we didn't have everything ready for our Dry Creek ballet premiere. At least I think we should call it a premiere in our advertising, don't you?"

"Advertising?" Lizette had a sinking feeling. She'd been focused on practicing and getting the costumes ready. "It's probably too late for advertising. I wasn't thinking. Newspapers usually need more notice. The performance is Friday."

"Edna will free up some place in the Miles City section of the paper," Mrs. Hargrove said. "It won't be much, but that's only one way to let people know. We can also put up posters."

"I don't have much money for printing and things like that," Lizette cautioned her. "I thought this would be a small performance since it's our first one."

"Don't you worry about a thing," Mrs. Hargrove said. "And, believe me, we won't have a small turnout."

Mrs. Hargrove should run for president, Lizette thought a few hours later. And not just of the USA. Mrs. Hargrove could run the world. She had arranged for Edna to do a review of the Nutcracker at a special dress rehearsal the cast would do Wednesday afternoon. That way people in the area would know about the Nutcracker and Lizette wouldn't have to pay for an ad. And, if that wasn't enough, the older woman also talked with Glory Curtis, the pastor's wife, and got an offer from the woman to create full-color posters to hang both at the hardware store and at several locations in Miles City.

"She's an artist, you know," Mrs. Hargrove confided to Lizette when she hung up the telephone. "She used to work as a police sketch artist—that's what she was doing when she first came to Dry Creek—and now she's gaining quite a reputation for her portraits."

"That's an unusual occupation for a pastor's wife. A police sketch artist?"

"Oh, well, she wasn't married to Matthew then," Mrs. Hargrove said. "Although she's always been an independent-minded woman, so it wouldn't make any difference to either of them if she was working for the police still—except for the fact that Matthew didn't like the thought of people shooting at her."

"Well, no, I suppose he wouldn't."

"I tell my daughter, Doris June, that a woman can be and do about anything in Dry Creek these days. She's always so worried about her career, but there's nothing to say she can't have a career right here."

"I hope your daughter does come home soon."

Lizette had heard about Mrs. Hargrove's plans to have her daughter come home and marry some local man from Judd. She hated to think that the older woman would be disappointed, but Lizette thought it was likely. "It must be hard when your daughter doesn't do what you want her to do."

"Ah, well," Mrs. Hargrove said. "A mother can hope."

Lizette was glad she was able to make her mother's dream come true even if her mother wasn't here to enjoy the fact with her. Sometimes, when the day was done and the streets of Dry Creek were quiet and dark, Lizette talked to her mother and told her all about what was happening with the Baker School of Ballet.

Sometimes, instead of pretending to talk to her mother, she actually called Madame Aprele and told her about what was happening. The odd thing was, she didn't exactly tell either woman the whole truth.

Lizette didn't want to disappoint them, so she made it sound as if the school was a real school and not just space in an old store. She made her students sound like real students and not just a few people she'd managed to talk into dressing up in costumes. She certainly wouldn't tell either of them that her premiere performance was going to be held in a barn or that both her Mouse King and her Nutcracker were hopeless at ballet.

One thing she could tell them, though, Lizette thought cheerfully, was that she was having someone from the local paper come to the dress rehearsal to write a review of the performance. That should make them both feel that her school was doing well.

Judd never thought he'd worry about the problems of being a Nutcracker. "If he's wearing a red military coat and black boots, you know he'd never agree to having some little girl stand in front when he's battling a mouse."

"Rat," Pete corrected him. "I'm a rat."

Pete was standing beside the fireplace that they had just moved over to the barn from Lizette's dance studio.

"When he's battling a large rodent," Judd corrected himself. "A Nutcracker just wouldn't do that. He's got more dignity."

Judd had gotten a better picture of the pride a Nutcracker would have when he'd seen the poster Glory Curtis had drawn. The poster showed the Nutcracker standing tall with the little girl, Clara, at his side. Glory had used both Judd and Lizette for models in the poster, and even though the sketch was in pencil, Judd swore it was the best likeness anyone had ever made of him, and the girl looked exactly like Lizette.

Judd figured people would know him as the Nut-

cracker for miles around. He didn't want people stopping him in the grocery store and demanding to know
what kind of man he was for letting a girl stand between
him and danger.

"But Clara owns the Nutcracker," Lizette protested.
She was draping an afghan over a wooden rocking chair
that Charley would sit in as the narrator. "She's only
protecting what is hers."

Judd had nothing to say to that. Actually, he didn't
want to say much to that. It made him feel pretty good.

Pete, however, had something to say. "It's only a nutcracker. Who'd be fool enough to risk getting a rat bite
just to save a wooden utensil? You could get rabies."

"He's her prince, that's why," Lizette said as she tucked
the back of the afghan into the arms of the rocker and then
stood back to look at her work. "There. That's straight."

Pete grunted. "It doesn't do any good to have a
prince if you're dead because of rabies."

"Don't worry," Lizette said as she moved the rocker
closer to the fireplace. "You'll do a good job of fighting him in the beginning and look very impressive."

"I could still switch and be the Nutcracker," Pete
suggested.

"Not on your life," Judd said. He knew Pete wasn't
so much dismayed at being a dead rodent as he was en-
vious of Judd for getting to kiss the ballerina. Well, actually, he hadn't kissed the ballerina since that first

time, but he figured one of these days Lizette would forget about the stage kiss and go for a real one.

"It's too late to make changes," Lizette said as she put a picture frame on the mantel of the fireplace. "We have the dress rehearsal at two o'clock tomorrow afternoon—I know it's not our usual time, but Edna needs to come then in order to get our review done for the paper."

"She's not going to take pictures, is she?" Pete asked.

Lizette shook her head. "I don't think so. She said there's not much room for the review even."

"Good," Pete said.

"You'll be able to get off work, won't you?" Lizette said to Pete.

Pete nodded.

"I know you don't have to worry," Lizette turned and said to Judd.

"One of the good things about owning your own place," Judd said as he helped Lizette place a small rug in front of the fireplace. "I'm free as a bird when it comes to my schedule."

Judd hoped she appreciated that he was a man with prospects. It didn't seem like she even noticed.

"I'll start with a quick rehearsal of the kids a couple of hours earlier, so I won't take either of you away from your work any longer than necessary," Lizette said as she straightened up after placing the rug.

"I can spare the time. I don't answer to anyone,"

Judd said as he brushed his hands on his jeans. Lizette wasn't even listening to his declaration of independence, so Judd gave it up. "As long as you've got plans for the kids, that'll give me a chance to run into Miles City without them. I want to check with the courts about their father. I'm wondering if anyone has asked him for more information about Barbara."

"You should have plenty of time to go to Miles City and back," Lizette said. "And if we finish early, I'll just put all of the kids to work cutting up those dried plums for the pastries I'm making."

"Really?" Pete brightened up. "The boys in the bunkhouse have been asking what kind of pastry these sugar-plum things are."

"It's like a cream-filled croissant with raisins, except there's a different kind of cream and the raisins are plums and it's not really croissant dough."

"But you don't need to go to the ballet to get one, do you?" Pete asked.

Lizette laughed. "I'm afraid so. I know you're hoping the others won't come, but that's the only way to get a sugar-plum pastry. Unless there are leftover ones after the ballet."

"There won't be any leftovers," Pete said.

"If you need any last-minute things from the store in Miles City, let me know since I'll be going in there anyway," Judd offered.

"I haven't thought of what to use as a cloth on the table where we'll be serving the pastries and punch," Lizette said. "Maybe you could buy some white silk fabric at the store—some of the washable kind would work best."

"I haven't seen any fabric stores in Miles City," Judd said. He didn't add that he wouldn't know silk if he saw it. He was more of a denim and flannel kind of a guy.

"Oh, I'm sure they must have a store that sells bolts of fabric," Lizette said. "You'll just have to ask around."

Judd decided he would have to take her word for it. She was probably right anyway. It was the kind of thing a woman would know.

Besides, Judd thought to himself, at least buying some silk would give him a good reason for going into Miles City apart from his vague unease. He was beginning to wish that Amanda and Bobby's father was already in the jail in Billings. Maybe there was something Judd could do to speed up the process if he went into Miles City and talked to whoever was in charge at the jail. Surely they could find room in the Billings jail if they put their minds to it.

Judd didn't know why he was feeling nervous. Everyone he had asked said that the jail in Miles City was built like a rock. A body had more chance of freezing to death inside their cell there than of actually making an escape.

Of course, Judd wasn't sure he was worried about the jail.

For all Judd knew, his unease might not even be about the kids' father. It might be about the upcoming ballet. Judd figured he knew his part as well as he was ever going to know it, and he was smart enough to realize that Lizette had organized everything, so he more or less stood still while she went twirling and dancing around him. He was more of a post than a dancer. Still, he was uneasy about the whole thing.

He'd never in his life performed in front of an audience. When he was riding in the rodeo, there had been an audience, but there was nothing required of the performers but to stay on the back of a horse. It was different than the ballet.

In this ballet, he was supposed to be the prince. Him—Judd Bowman. He knew that Lizette didn't have many contenders for the role, but still. He'd never figured he was a prince kind of a guy. He was more like the guy out in the stables who took care of everything while the prince was inside talking to people and impressing the princess.

If Judd had known that the Nutcracker was more than a utensil, he'd have thought twice about volunteering for the role. Even now, if any man but Pete stepped forward and said he wanted to play the role, Judd would be tempted to let him.

A man could just pretend to be something he wasn't for so long in life. Judd figured his limit would be Saturday. He hoped he would get through the ballet with no problems. Then he could go back to counting out his nails so he could finish working on that fence of his like the solitary guy he was meant to be.

There wasn't anything wrong with building fences, he reminded himself. He needed those fences, and that's what he'd started out to do that day he'd come to town with the kids. This whole ballet business had just been a distraction. He needed to get back to business. Besides, the whole world would be a better place if people had more fences.

Chapter Fourteen

It was only six o'clock, but Lizette was wide awake. She was lying in her bed in the back of her dance studio and looking at the hands of the clock on her nightstand. For a moment, she thought her alarm must have gone off, but it hadn't. It wasn't scheduled to go off for another hour.

Lizette had just had a dream about mice escaping into the audience and the Nutcracker's hat falling off his head. The reason she was awake was that she was having performance jitters. She hadn't had those in years. The odd thing was that she wasn't even worried about the dancing. She could dance Clara's role in her sleep, and she'd simplified everyone else's steps so they would look fine even if they forgot everything she'd taught them. Clara did all of the true ballet dancing.

No, she wasn't fretting about the dancing; she was worried about more basic things—things like the tin soldier dying in the wrong place or the mice giggling in the middle of their fierce attack.

Or the Nutcracker forgetting how to stage a kiss and giving her the real thing. Not that she was worried about thinking the kiss would mean anything. She'd given herself that speech enough times the last time it happened that she didn't think she'd fall for that illusion again. Even if their lips did happen to meet, she would know it was just an acting kiss.

But it could still fluster her so that she would forget some steps in the performance. Since she was really the only one dancing, that could be a problem. She was going to have to remember to tell Judd again that their stage kiss didn't require any physical contact. The audience couldn't see if their lips touched or not. They were supposed to air kiss beside their lips, not on their lips.

Maybe she should draw him a diagram, Lizette thought as she stretched and threw back the covers.

Ohh, it was cold. Lizette had the heat on in her room at the back of the studio, but she had kept it low. Until she knew how much money she would be making each month, she didn't want to spend too much extra on heat. That was an incentive to get more students if nothing else was.

Lizette reached under the quilt that covered her bed and pulled out the sweatpants and sweatshirt that she'd put there last night. Her neighbor Linda, at the café, had taught her that trick. When it was cold out, you took your clothes for the next day to bed with you and they were warm when you got up. Of course, Linda recommended putting them just under the top blanket instead of between the sheets. That way, she assured Lizette, the clothes didn't get wrinkled.

Lizette pulled the sweatpants on.

She then quickly pulled on the sweatshirt, telling herself she should just go over and take another look at the stage they had made in the barn. She wanted to see what everything looked like in the muted light of morning. This lighting would be the closest to the subdued light they'd have on their actual performance and Lizette didn't want to miss any chance to see how the shadows would fall. She wasn't sure how the shadows could help her, but knowledge always made one better prepared.

After all, she told herself as she walked to her stove and turned the tea kettle on, her very first ballet production was going to be reviewed this afternoon. She hadn't realized quite how important that was until she had talked with Madame Aprele a few days ago and told her about the upcoming review.

Of course, she hadn't told Madame Aprele that the

review was going to run in a section of the paper called "Dry Creek Tidbits" or that Edna Best, the woman reviewing the ballet, obviously didn't recognize the Nutcracker and was, by her own admission, more comfortable covering the bait and poundage reports during fishing season.

Lizette saw no reason to dismay her former teacher when the basic facts themselves were encouraging. Her ballet performance was scheduled in a large local community center, her dress rehearsal was Wednesday at two o'clock, during which time a reviewer would be present to critique the performance, and the Snow Queen was predicting a good audience turnout for the actual performance.

Madame Aprele was ecstatic with the news, and Lizette told herself she should just focus on the good things that she had told Madame Aprele.

It took Lizette ten more minutes to wash her face and fix her hair. She thought about putting some makeup on just to help keep her face warmer, but decided against it. Then she put her wool coat on and wrapped a knit scarf around her ears and neck. She had put a tea bag in her cup of hot water a few minutes ago, and now she poured the tea into a thermal mug so she could take it with her to the barn.

The air was cold outside. There was no fresh snow, but the snow from yesterday was still on the streets of

Dry Creek. It had been tramped down and was starting to be slippery.

The day promised to be gray, and Lizette wondered if she'd gone out too soon. The hardware store was still closed, as was the café. There was a bathroom light on in the parsonage next to the church, but there were no other lights in the houses along the street. Most people had sense enough to stay in bed until the sun had a chance to warm up the day.

Lizette decided maybe she had the heat too low in her room. It barely seemed any colder outside than it had been inside. She would be glad to have the tea to drink while she looked around the stage.

The windows in the barn were covered with frost, and thin strips of snow sat on top of the door rim. The main double door was wide enough for a farmer's wagon to pass through it. The walls of the barn had been painted the usual red, and the trim was white. A wide slab of cement stood in front of the door to help with the mud.

The place might be humble compared to other performance centers, but it was large, clean and sturdy. It even had a heating system. Apparently Mr. Elkton had installed heating in the building after the town started using it for their meeting center. Of course, it took a long time to heat up the huge building, so he had suggested she turn the heat on low several days before the performance.

Lizette had turned the heat up to fifty degrees yesterday, and she was looking forward to seeing what the air was like inside the barn.

"Oh," Lizette muttered as she looked at the barn door. When she'd turned the heat on yesterday, she'd also locked the front door to the barn. She had brought the trunk over that held the props and costumes and she thought the sight of all those might tempt someone to experiment with them. And maybe it had, because now the door was most decidedly unlocked. It wasn't unlatched, but clearly someone had gone inside since Lizette had been here yesterday.

Of course, Lizette told herself as she opened the door and stepped into the barn, she supposed that half of the adults in Dry Creek had keys to the barn. One of them might have wanted to check to be sure the heat was on.

Lizette turned on the overhead light. She was enough of a city woman to want the lights instead of the shadows until she figured out if anything was missing.

The Christmas tree was there, right in the middle of the area they had decided on as the stage. The cardboard fireplace stood next to the wooden rocking chair. The old Christmas stockings that Mrs. Hargrove had hung on the stairs leading up to the hayloft were still tied in place. Folding chairs lined the edges of the barn and a table was sitting at the far end of the barn where they were going to put the pastries and punch.

No one had moved anything big.

It was the bathrobe, Lizette decided after she looked around. All of the costumes and props were still in the trunk except for the heavy bathrobe that the narrator wore. Maybe Charley had come to get it for some reason. Or Mrs. Hargrove might have decided it needed a good washing and taken it with her. It certainly was nothing someone would steal.

Lizette told herself it really didn't matter as she walked over to the small panel that ran the sound system. A bathrobe was the one costume that she could easily replace. She bet there were a dozen old bathrobes around that the men of Dry Creek would donate if she made the need known. Especially if she promised the bathrobe owner wouldn't have to actually dance in the ballet along with his robe.

Lizette selected the Nutcracker audiocassette, inserted it into the panel, and turned the volume on low.

Pete Denning kept saying that he was willing to do whatever she needed to help with the ballet, and he could probably find a bathrobe in that bunkhouse where he lived that looked as warm and comfortable as the one Charley had been using. Of course, the reason Pete was so helpful was because he was hoping she'd go out with him when the ballet was over.

If Pete had kept the role of the Nutcracker, he would have studied up on the proper way to give a stage kiss.

So far, Lizette had been able to gently refuse his requests for dates, explaining that it was not proper for her to date one of her students. Pete had offered to quit right then if she'd go out with him instead. Fortunately, Lizette had talked him out of that idea, as well. But he was bound to ask her out again after the Nutcracker was finished, and she didn't know what she would say.

The sounds of Tchaikovsky's music filled the old barn. It truly was beautiful, soaring music Lizette thought to herself. Whoever had set up the speaker system had done a professional job. Several speakers hung from the rafters and several more hung either beside the hayloft or on the other side of the barn by where the refreshment table stood.

If the barn were a few degrees warmer, Lizette would be tempted to take her coat off and dance awhile. If nothing else, the sounds of Tchaikovsky would bring enough culture to the people of Dry Creek to reward them for coming to the ballet.

Lizette drank the last swallow of her tea before she walked back to the door and opened it a crack. She looked across the road and saw that a light was now on in Linda's café. Good, Lizette thought, she would forget about the cereal in her cupboard and have a proper breakfast in the café this morning. After all, it was an important day. A critic from the press was going to come and review her performance.

The blinds were half-drawn on the café windows and there were no customers other than Lizette. The floor was a black-and-white pattern and the tables and chairs had a fifties' look about them. A large glass counter filled the back wall. Linda had added a counter recently to sell more baked goods.

There was a phone call just as Linda was bringing Lizette's order out.

Linda set Lizette's plate of food down on the counter and answered the phone.

"Some telemarketer," Linda had said thirty seconds later as she put the phone back on the hook and picked Lizette's plate up again. "Asking about a taxi in Dry Creek. Anyone from here to Wyoming knows there's no taxi in Dry Creek."

"Why would they call the café anyway?"

Linda shrugged as she put Lizette's plate in front of her. "We're the only business in the phone book with Dry Creek in our name. People get confused."

"Well, just as long as it's not Edna Best from the newspaper."

Linda snorted. "Edna was born out this way. She'd be the last to call for a taxi."

Lizette figured it probably was a telemarketer then. In any event, she wasn't going to worry about it. She had a plate of golden-brown French toast in front of her, and it was sprinkled with blueberries and raspberries.

Linda went to the kitchen and came back with a bowl of oatmeal for herself along with an apple and a small glass of orange juice.

"These frozen berries are the best," Lizette said.

"I'm trying out a new brand," Linda said as she sat down across from Lizette.

The two ate in silence for a few minutes. Then Lizette fretted aloud about the newspaper critic. "A review can make or break a production."

"Don't worry. Edna will be positive. She's probably never even been to a ballet."

"Still, it doesn't hurt to be prepared."

"Well, she's liked her coffee strong and black as long as I've known her. Having a full cup will go a long way to giving her a positive impression since it's so cold outside," Linda said as Lizette finished up her French toast. "I'll fix up a big thermal jug for you to come get around one o'clock. And I still have a few of those chocolate chip pecan cookies you made. We'll put those on a plate for her. That should take care of Edna. Did I tell you my afternoon business has picked up since I've started selling cookies to go with the coffee?"

Last week, Linda had offered Lizette meals in exchange for baked goods to sell in the café. So far, Lizette had made individual apple coffeecakes and the cookies.

"I'm thinking I'll try some pies next," Lizette said

as she pushed her plate away. "Maybe cherry and apple with a special order possible for chocolate pecan for the holidays."

Linda sat across the table from Lizette with her glass of orange juice in her hand. "I can sell all the baked goods you give me. You can make money in addition to your meals. We might even make up a batch of fruit cakes."

"The people of Dry Creek sure do like their baked goods."

Linda nodded as she picked up her apple. "They need to eat more fruits and vegetables, but you'll never convince these ranch hands around here. If it's not meat or bread, they think it's not food. I'm surprised you haven't started getting marriage proposals. I guess they're all giving you a month or so to settle in before they start to pester you with their pleading."

Lizette laughed. "If they like good cooking, I would think they'd be stopping at your door instead. I don't know when I've had such good French toast."

"It's the bread," Linda said. "I use sweet bread. Besides, I've refused them all so many times they've stopped asking."

"Don't you want to get married?"

Linda finished chewing her bite of apple. "I was engaged once. That was enough."

Lizette didn't think the other woman could be over twenty-two. "What happened?"

"He decided he wanted to be a music star instead," Linda said as she leaned back in her chair and put the rest of the apple on her plate. "Life here in Dry Creek wasn't good enough for him."

"Oh, I'm sorry."

"Don't be. The funny thing is that he's making it. I've started to hear his songs on the radio. He's even doing some big tour in Europe."

"But he could have taken you with him!"

Linda smiled. "He offered a while back. I just didn't want to go. Who wants to be the wife that keeps him back? And then there are the fans. I didn't want to share my husband with them. No, I'm better off here in the café."

Lizette noticed that the other woman's voice was too bright and brittle to be convincing. "Well, if there's ever anything I can do, let me know."

"Thanks," Linda said as she stood up. "But there's nothing anyone can do. We make our choices in life and then we live with them."

"But have you talked to him since or written him a letter or anything?"

Linda shrugged. "What would I say? Sorry you're becoming a star. I miss the old you. No, he's gone on and I've stayed the same."

"Well," Lizette said as she, too, stood up from the table. She noticed the sun had fully risen. It was a new day. "Maybe there will be a nice young rancher move into town and you'll come to like him."

"There is Judd Bowman," Linda said as she stopped walking to the back of the café and turned to face Lizette. "He seems nice enough."

Lizette swallowed. "Yes, he does."

"Hmm," Linda said as her eyes started to twinkle. "He does seem a little preoccupied lately, though. I'm not sure I could get his full attention."

"He's just worried about the ballet."

Linda grinned. "Is that what he's worried about?"

"Well, he's probably still worried about his cousin and the kids' father, too."

"I don't know—all I hear him muttering about lately is Pete Denning and how he gets all of the attention in those classes of yours. If I didn't know better, I would say he was jealous."

"I try to give all of my students my full attention," Lizette said. "It's just that some of them are—"

"—more difficult," Linda supplied helpfully. "More independent. More disturbing."

"Yes," Lizette said. She was glad someone understood. "Judd is all of those."

Linda nodded. "Good."

"I don't know if it's good. It does make the ballet more difficult."

"But doesn't it make life more interesting?"

"Maybe," Lizette admitted. "But right now I have a critic to prepare for and plum filling to make."

"The kids can help with the plum filling, and Mrs. Hargrove and I will help you with the custard. I've never made a cream filling, but Mrs. Hargrove will know how."

"You have those kettles with the thick bottoms," Lizette said. "That's the key right there."

"How many pastries do you figure you'll need?"

"Mrs. Hargrove figures we'll need twenty dozen."

"Two hundred and forty!"

Lizette nodded. "She says we're going to bring in crowds from all around."

"I'd better get my salads made for lunch right now then, so I can clear the kitchen for the custard. Mrs. Hargrove will be over any minute."

"Be sure she remembers to come over to the performance area in time to get ready for Edna." Lizette refused to call the place a barn. From today until the night of the ballet, it was a performance center.

"She'll be there. I think she's excited to be the Ice Queen."

Lizette smiled. "She's the Snow Queen. She's in charge of the snowflakes."

"Then you have nothing to worry about," Linda said.

Lizette repeated the words to herself as she left the café. She had nothing to worry about. The people of Dry Creek would be kind critics. They were looking for entertainment, not perfection. Everything would be just fine.

Chapter Fifteen

Nothing was fine. Lizette's watch was missing. Which meant the schedule was all off. The kids were still at the table cutting up dried plums, and they should be in their costumes if they were going to practice before the dress rehearsal. Plus, Linda had just come over with a message saying that Pete had been out working with the cattle and had run into a bit of a problem, but that Lizette wasn't to worry. He would be there in no time.

It wasn't until Linda mentioned that Pete was late that Lizette looked for her watch. She couldn't believe she hadn't known how much time had passed. She'd been busy diagramming the steps to a stage kiss and it had taken her longer than she had anticipated. That's why she hadn't noticed she didn't have her watch with her. She'd left it on the cardboard fireplace before she'd gone over to the café for breakfast.

"I'm sure it was there," Lizette said as she started walking over to the stage area.

"Maybe the mice took it," Amanda offered. She had followed Lizette over from the table. The little girl had a dish towel wrapped around her neck for an apron and a piece of twine holding her hair in place. She was licking a spoon that had plum mixture on it. "Or maybe the big rat that lives in the fireplace took it. He's scary."

"The mice were over there with us cutting up dried plums and the rat better be in his pickup driving here." Lizette checked to see that the mice really were still at the table before she looked around again. There weren't any cracks big enough for a watch to fall into, and the furniture in the stage area didn't have any pillows or other hidden areas. "Maybe someone came in and borrowed it."

"More likely someone stole it," Linda replied. "You could report it to the Billings police. Charley is probably at the hardware store by now, and I know he's itching to call something in now that Sheriff Wall is out of town and has designated him and his son as the men to watch Dry Creek."

"I don't think anyone would steal it," Lizette said. She'd only paid twenty dollars for the watch. It wouldn't be worth it for anyone to steal it to resell it.

Linda shrugged. "Well, Mrs. Hargrove is making some bread dough for hamburger buns for me—I'm running low on buns again. But she's going to be here any minute."

Lizette nodded. Judd wasn't back from Miles City, either. He was going to stop at the jail and talk to whoever was in charge there and then he was going to locate four yards of white silk material for her. He should be back any minute, as well. And, when he did get back, she wanted to go over her diagram with him and explain once again that there is no physical contact in a stage kiss.

"So what time is it again?" Lizette asked Linda.

"My watch isn't accurate, either," Linda said. "I was working with it to use it as an oven timer, so I'm not sure if it's twelve forty-five or one forty-five."

"Oh, it can't be one forty-five," Lizette said. "Edna Best is supposed to be here before two and—"

The sound of a car honking came from outside the door.

"That must be Pete," Lizette said hopefully. Or maybe Judd. Or Mrs. Hargrove. Anybody but Edna Best. They weren't at all ready for the reviewer to be here. They weren't even in costume.

"I'll go get that coffee," Linda said as she looked out the window and turned to the door. "And remember, she's one of us. She won't go hard on you, and she's early, anyway. Maybe you should send her over for a cup of coffee."

"Hellooo," a woman's voice called from the outside.

Lizette took a deep breath and put a smile on her face. Then she walked to the door of the barn and opened it up. "Welcome. You must be Edna Best."

The woman nodded. She was a short, plump woman wrapped in a hooded parka. "I wasn't sure where the performance was."

"We have some posters up in the hardware store, and we're making a sign that says 'Nutcracker' to point people to us," Lizette said, realizing she had also forgotten that they needed programs for the evening of the ballet. She hoped that Edna wouldn't ask to see one. That would show her right away that they were amateurs.

"Most folks will know where it is anyway if we say the Elkton barn," Edna said as she stepped inside. "The only question they'll have is about the cost. I didn't see the cost mentioned anywhere in the notes I have so far."

"Cost?" Lizette said. "We weren't planning to charge."

"Of course you've got to charge," Edna said as she looked around inside. "Maybe not much, but enough to pay your expenses. I know props and costumes don't come cheap."

"Most of the costumes are mine, and my former ballet teacher is lending us the props and some more costumes. I'm planning to send her money for postage when I return them to her, but that's not much of an expense."

"Ah," Edna said as she took a small notepad out of her black purse. "That might be a lead. 'Big-city ballet teacher does favor for local teacher.'"

"I don't think Madame Aprele would want to be the feature in your story," Lizette said. "She doesn't like to be written up in the media unless it's for her dancing."

"Madame Aprele?" Edna said as she wrote the name in her book. "That's an interesting name. She's not in the witness protection program or anything, is she? I hear they let you make up your own name. We had a rancher some years ago down by Forsyth that turned out to be in the witness protection program. He never wanted to be in the paper, either. We weren't even sure if we should put his obituary in the paper when he died. We did, of course, but we wondered."

"I don't know if that's her real name," Lizette said as she tried to steer the reviewer toward the folding chairs she had set up earlier around the stage area. "I've always called her that, and I've known her for more than fifteen years."

Edna let herself be led.

"I'm sorry it's not warmer in here," Lizette said. "Linda's going to bring some coffee and a cookie over for you shortly."

"I heard she's been serving cookies lately. When the guys in the newsroom found out I was coming out here, they all told me to bring back cookies if I could. I hear she's got a baker making cookies for her."

"That's me," Lizette said. "I bake a little in my spare time."

"Now that's the hook for my story," Edna said as she settled herself into a folding chair next to the chair Lizette had been sitting in when she was diagramming the stage kiss. "Baker Turns to Ballet for—" Edna paused. "Why would you say you turned to ballet from baking? For inspiration? For profit?"

"It's been my dream," Lizette said as she tried to figure out a way to get her kissing diagram back before Edna noticed it sitting on the chair next to her.

Maybe the best approach was the most direct, Lizette thought as she reached over to pick up the diagram. "Let me just get this out of your way. It's nothing—just some stage directions."

Lizette willed herself to stop. She always talked too much when she was nervous. "Nothing. It's nothing."

"I had no idea you had stage directions in a ballet," Edna said as she looked up from her notebook and frowned. "I told the guys in the newsroom that I didn't know enough to cover this story."

"Oh, don't worry," Lizette said. "I can tell you anything you want to know."

"They only sent me here because I'm a woman."

"Well, I'm glad you came anyway," Lizette said as she sat down beside Edna. "Just ask me any questions you want. I can tell you everything you need."

Edna's face brightened. "That's kind of you. Not everyone takes the time to explain things. First, tell me about these stage directions. What were you mapping out? The battle with the mice?"

Lizette wished she could lie, but she couldn't. "The kiss."

Edna's face brightened even more. "Who's kissing who?"

"The Nutcracker kisses Clara."

Edna frowned. "Isn't the Nutcracker, well, a nutcracker? And isn't Clara a little girl? I did some research on the Internet just to get the basic plot. I only got the start of the ballet, but—"

"When Clara kills the Mouse King, she turns into a young lady and the Nutcracker turns into a prince. That's when they kiss."

"My, how romantic!" Edna said as she wrote in her notebook. "People around here love a romance. So, tell me, who plays the Nutcracker again?"

"Judd Bowman."

"He's the guy out on the old Jenkins place, isn't he?"

Lizette nodded.

"So the stage directions are for him? On how to kiss?"

"Well, sort of. You see a stage kiss is different than a real kiss—"

Lizette heard another set of tires in the distance. Now, that should be the sound of one of her dancers coming.

The door opened and Linda came inside along with a gust of snowy wind. "There's a regular convention out there."

"Is it Pete or Judd?"

"Neither," Linda said as she brought the thermos of coffee over to Edna. "It's a taxi."

"But there are no taxis here," Lizette said, even as she began to wonder if—

There was the sound of a honking horn and the slamming of a car door outside. Lizette walked to the window. The heat had been on long enough that a small corner of the window was now clear of frost. It was a large enough piece of window that Lizette could see a woman, covered from head to toe in black wool and black scarves. The only color anywhere was a lavender feather boa that the woman had flung around her shoulders.

Madame Aprele was outside.

Lizette hurried to the door even though she wanted to hurry in the other direction and find a place to hide. She opened the door. "Madame. What a surprise! A pleasant surprise!"

"Oh, Lizette." Madame Aprele turned toward Lizette with relief in her voice. Then she started unwinding all of the black scarves and walking toward the open door. "I'm glad I found you. This man was trying to tell me that this barn is the town's performance center. What kind of an old fool does he take me for? I'm so glad you're here so you can show me the way to where you're doing your dress rehearsal for that reviewer. I came to lend my moral support. Newspaper people can be so difficult."

By the time Madame Aprele stopped talking, she had unwound all of the scarves from her head and was fully inside the barn.

"Dear me," was all she said as she looked around.

"Madame Aprele," Lizette said as she held out her arm for the many scarves. "I'm touched that you came all of the way from Seattle. If you'd like me to take your scarves, I can."

Madame Aprele gave Lizette the black scarves. "You're rehearsing here?"

Lizette nodded as she held out her elbow for Madame Aprele to take. "Yes, and I'll take you down for a front-row seat right next to Edna Best, the woman who is going to review us."

"You're rehearsing in a barn?" Madame Aprele asked. "When do you move it to the performance center?"

"The barn *is* the performance center," Lizette said as she started walking Madame Aprele down to the chairs next to the stage.

"But what about the cows?" Madame Aprele said as she sat down in the chair next to Edna Best.

"You have cows in the ballet, too?" Edna asked as she wrote something in her notebook.

"No, there are no cows," Lizette said as she stood beside the two seated women. "Now, if you'll excuse me, I need to get my dancers ready. Madame Aprele, let me introduce you to Edna Best, who's going to review our performance today. Maybe you could answer any questions she has?"

Both women nodded to her and then to each other.

Well, Lizette thought as she stepped away, she'd done all she could. Even if one of her dancers didn't show up, she could deal with it now. All of the things in her nightmare could happen and it wouldn't even faze her now. Madame Aprele had come and seen that she was a fraud.

Her mother's old enemy and her new friend had seen that all of the things Lizette had said about her little dance school were nothing more than the longing in her heart that it be so. The performance center was a barn. Her dance students were over at a table eating a mixture of dried plums and sugar. None of them were in costume. And the only reason any of them were even her students was because they wanted to wear those costumes. The reviewer who was going to write about the ballet, although she was kind, had never even seen a ballet performance before.

There was no way for it to be worse than it was.

Lizette squared her shoulders. She had absolutely nothing to fear now. Let the ballet begin.

Chapter Sixteen

Judd Bowman wished silk had never been invented. Or women. Or both of them. If he hadn't decided to track down some white silk cloth for Lizette before he stopped at the jail to check about Neal Strong, the kids' father, he wouldn't have wasted two hours of valuable time that he could have spent out looking for the escaped prisoner alongside the sheriff's department.

Neal had escaped yesterday afternoon.

Someone had decided that there was room in the Billings jail for Neal and had gone to Miles City to get him in a patrol car. On the way there, Neal complained that he needed to use a restroom. Unfortunately, no one checked to be sure Neal's handcuffs were secure before they escorted him to the restroom. When a backup patrol car came to investigate why there was no response to a radio message, the officers found one of their own unconscious on the floor of the restroom, and Neal, along with the officer's gun, nowhere to be found.

Judd demanded to know why no one had called him last night with the news, only to be told that they were trying to reach Sheriff Wall in Colorado to inform him of what had happened.

Judd pressed the gas pedal on his pickup a little farther down. The police in Billings thought Neal was more likely to head for a drug dealer or the border than his children, but Judd wasn't so sure. He wasn't going to take any chances.

Judd relaxed a little when he saw Pete's pickup in front of the barn where the ballet rehearsal was going to happen. The cowboy would see to the kids' safety if their father was around.

Judd looked at the clock on his dashboard. Speaking of the ballet, he was late. He hoped the extra yards of white silk he'd bought would be enough to make Lizette forgive him.

It hadn't been easy to find silk in Miles City. Judd had had to buy it from a secondhand store owner who called someone he knew who had some white silk left from an old customer who had been using the stuff to make parachutes—or maybe it was bags for parachutes. Neither store owner could remember. They did remember it had been extra-strong silk, guaranteed to hold a hundred pounds, or maybe it was two hundred pounds. They couldn't remember how much.

Judd assured them the silk only had to be strong enough to hold a punch cup, and that he would take it as soon as the other man could get it there. He only hoped it wasn't nylon instead of silk. No one was really sure on that point, either.

Lizette was still waiting to begin the performance. Linda and Mrs. Hargrove had helped clean the faces of her younger dancers and slipped their costumes over their heads. Charley had fussed about his missing bathrobe so much that Lizette had given him a big towel to wrap around his shoulders. Then Pete had walked in a few minutes ago with a bruise on his cheek, muttering something about a stubborn cow. Lizette had asked him what happened, but he shrugged and said he'd tell her later.

"The show must go on," Pete said with a grin as he took his Mouse King costume off the chair where Lizette had laid it and started toward the stairway leading up to the hay loft. "I'll be right back."

"Oh, you can change down here," Lizette said. She hadn't wanted to send the children up to the cold hay loft to change, so she and Charley had hung a blanket in a corner of the barn.

But Pete was already halfway up the stairs with his tail dragging behind him.

Lizette herself was in her ballet slippers and her yellow dress.

"I can fill in for the Nutcracker," Mrs. Hargrove offered. The older woman had changed into her billowing Snow Queen costume and was chatting with Madame Aprele and Edna Best. "I think I have his lines memorized from watching him practice with you."

Charley was sitting in his rocking chair next to the Christmas tree. "The whole thing?"

Mrs. Hargrove nodded.

"So you'd do the Nutcracker kiss?" Edna Best asked as she pulled her notebook back out of her purse.

"Oh, no," Mrs. Hargrove said, and then chuckled. "I see you're still looking for that headline."

Edna smiled and shrugged. "Nothing ever happens around here. I was hoping maybe I could get a news story in the regular part of the paper as well as a review in the Dry Creek Tidbits section."

"Surely it's news that a ballet is going to take place in a barn," Madame Aprele offered helpfully. The older woman no longer seemed as shocked about everything and was actually giving Edna some valuable pointers on how to review the ballet. "In Seattle, that would be a headline."

"Barns are not news around here," Edna said. "We have so many of them."

"Well, you'll have to wait for Judd to get here to

stage the kiss," Mrs. Hargrove said. "Although I must say, he seems to have a mind of his own about how a kiss should go on."

"That's why I drew him a diagram," Lizette said. "He just needs to see how to do it."

Charley snorted. "Whoever heard of a diagram for a kiss?"

There was a thud up in the hayloft that sounded as if Pete was taking off his boots.

Edna was writing notes. "Could you tell me more about what's lacking in the way the Nutcracker kisses?"

"Oh, I didn't say anything was lacking," Lizette said. She hoped the boot thud meant that Pete was almost in his costume. "And I don't really think you should be quoting me on this. I mean, I'm not an expert on kissing or anything. It's just for the ballet scene."

Lizette decided there was really no need to wait for the Nutcracker to arrive before they began the production. "Charley can just read the Nutcracker's lines."

"I can do the Nutcracker's kissing, too," Charley said firmly. "In my day and age, we didn't do any of this stage-kissing stuff. That's just for Hollywood types."

"How do you know? You've never kissed a Hollywood type," Mrs. Hargrove said.

"Now, how do you know who I've kissed and who I haven't kissed?" Charley said with his chin in the air.

"Well, I've known you all your life."

"That doesn't mean you know all about me. I could still surprise you yet."

"Don't think I couldn't surprise you, too," Mrs. Hargrove retorted.

My goodness, Lizette thought, what was wrong with the two of them?

Someone cleared his throat loudly from the sidelines. It must be Pete coming down the stairs, Lizette thought as she looked up.

"Speaking of surprises," Pete said calmly as he stood very still.

Pete hadn't changed into his costume, although he did have another bruise on his face. Still wearing his work jeans and a flannel shirt, he was standing at the top of the stairs with his arms in the air. There were shadows, but there was enough light to see the gun that was being held to the back of Pete's head as well as the man behind him holding the gun.

There was silence for a moment.

"There's my bathrobe," Charley finally said.

Lizette felt two pairs of little arms circle around her legs.

"That's my dad," Bobby whispered as he tightened his grip on Lizette's legs.

"You've been hiding up there all day?" Lizette said. She tried to make her voice sound normal and conversational. She didn't want the children terrified any more than they already were. "No wonder the door to the barn was unlocked. After all that time, you must be hungry."

"I'm not hungry. I have a headache. I've been trying to sleep, except you have that awful music playing and it's making my eyes cross."

The man did look pale, even in the shadows.

"That's Tchaikovsky!" Madame Aprele protested. "He's famous. He's never given anyone a headache!"

"I prefer a fiddle," the man said. "Something with some spirit."

Madame Aprele opened her mouth to say something and then thought better of it and closed it again.

Lizette agreed there was no reason to argue music with a man holding a gun. "I'll be happy to turn the music off, and then maybe you can go back and lie down and have a good rest."

The man snorted. "Nice try, but I think I'll stay right here where I can see everybody. Like you, old man." He pointed at Charley. "I see you reaching inside your coat pocket for something. You got a gun in there?"

Charley held up his open hands. "No gun. I was reaching for an antacid. Stress is killing me."

"Well, you keep your hands out of your pockets." The man nudged Pete to start walking down the stairs. "You all keep your hands where I can see them. We have a situation here."

"We don't need to have a situation," Lizette said as

she put her own hands out in full view. "If you just put the gun down, no one needs to get hurt."

"You'd like that, wouldn't you? You always were looking out for yourself first," the man said. "I remember you from the gas station. No room for a poor man like me to ride with you when anyone could see you had enough room. Someone like you thinks they're better than me. Well, you're not better than me now. Not when I've got the gun."

"I don't think I'm better than anyone," Lizette said. "I just want everyone to be safe."

There was an awkward silence as everyone thought about being safe.

"You must be Neal Strong," Edna finally said. She had her hands out in front of her, as well. "I've heard about you. Something about a wrongful arrest."

"You bet it was wrongful!"

"Well, maybe you'd like to put down the gun and tell me about it. I'm a reporter with the newspaper. If we work at getting your story out there, maybe there's a chance for you."

"The only chance for me is this," Neal said as he nodded toward the gun he held in his hand.

Pete and Neal had reached the bottom of the stairs, but no one started to breathe normally.

Even with no breath left in their lungs, they all gasped when the door to the barn started to open.

Judd held himself perfectly still. He'd come up to the door earlier and heard some of what was happening inside. He'd run over to the café and asked Linda to call the police in Billings and tell them their man was armed and in the big barn in Dry Creek. Then he'd run back to the barn door.

"I know I'm late," Judd said as he stepped into the main area of the barn. He had the white silk under one arm. "I had a hard time finding the silk and—"

Judd broke off his words, hoping he sounded genuinely surprised. "Well, who's this?"

Judd already knew who the man was, but he didn't want to give Neal any reason to be suspicious that Judd had notified the authorities.

"I'm the kids' dad," Neal said as waved his gun around. "You must be that cousin of Barbara's? You look a lot like her."

Judd felt his smile tighten. "You've seen Barbara?"

Neal nodded. "Tracked her down. I told her she had no right to leave the kids off somewhere. I'm their dad. I say where they're supposed to be."

Judd knew he shouldn't argue with the man, but he didn't like the scared look Amanda was giving him.

Judd took a casual step closer to the kids. "Bobby and Amanda are with me for now. They're no trouble. No need to bother yourself with them."

"You and Barbara would like that, wouldn't you?"

Neal sneered. "You're two of a kind. Bowmans both of you. You're spoiling the kids."

So that's what family is, Judd thought. Hearing your name coupled with someone else's in a sneer and not even minding it because it meant someone else was in the thick of it with you. What do you know? He did have a family.

"They're good kids." Judd took another step closer to Amanda and Bobby. He figured the gun could go off at any minute, but if it did he had some things to say to some people before he died. "I'm not nearly good enough for those kids of yours, but if they were mine, I'd be proud of it. They're part of my family and I love them both."

Judd half expected the gun to go off when he said he loved the kids. Maybe Neal Strong didn't hear him. The words echoed in Judd's own ears, but that might be because he'd rarely even said he *liked* anyone in his life. He'd certainly never admitted to loving anyone. Love had never been for a man like him. Judd wasn't sure what love was, so he couldn't say for sure that's what he felt when he looked at those two kids holding on to Lizette's legs, but it must be. He was willing to die to protect them. That had to be something close to the love that made a family a family.

All three pairs of eyes—Lizette's and the two kids'—looked up at him.

Judd blinked. He wondered what was happening to the air around here that a man's eyes could tear up just looking at someone.

Judd took the final step that brought him next to Lizette and the kids.

"Now ain't that touching," Neal drawled as Amanda and Bobby left Lizette's legs and wrapped themselves around Judd.

Judd resisted the urge to bend down and lift the children into his arms. Instead, he gently guided both children to the back of his legs so that there would be less of them to be targets if Neal was as unsettled as he looked.

Judd forced himself to shrug. "It's still cold in here. They just like to wrap themselves around something warm. That's all."

Neal snorted. "You don't fool me. I don't let go of what's mine all that easy. Just ask Barbara."

"I've been wanting to talk to Barbara," Judd said casually. "Do you know where I can reach her?"

Neal just laughed. "You ain't getting nothing out of me."

"I'd be willing to pay," Judd said smoothly.

"I've got money."

"I wasn't thinking of cash," Judd said. He hoped the police speculation that Neal had been going through drug withdrawal was correct. "I've got some white stuff out in the pickup that might interest you."

"What is it?" Neal said.

Judd saw the look in Neal's eyes and knew he had him. Hook, line and sinker. "Not something you'd want me to announce right out here in the open."

"Bring it in."

Judd shrugged. "If you were interested in it, I'd throw in the pickup, as well. You might want to get out of here before anyone knows you're here."

Neal took a few steps closer to the door, turning as he walked so that everyone was still in his range of vision.

"I need your keys."

Judd tossed him the keys to his pickup.

"Where's the stuff?"

"In the back of the pickup, alongside the hay bales I have in there. I'm not sure what side it's on."

"What? You can't be too careful with the stuff, man."

"I'm sure you'll take care of it." Judd watched as the man walked even closer to the door.

"Is it good?" Neal asked when he had his back at the door.

"Pure as snow," Judd said as he watched the other man open the door and slide outside.

Judd counted to two. He figured it would take the man that long to get off the steps. "Everybody out the back window."

Pete was already with him on this one and had

opened the back window already. The cold air swept across the barn, but no one noticed.

Judd rushed over to the door and locked it from the inside. It would take the man a while to find the key that had let him into the barn in the first place.

"The little ones first," Madame Aprele said as she lifted Amanda into Pete's arms.

Pete lifted the little girl out the window. Then he lifted Bobby.

Charley brought over a chair for the women, and one by one they climbed up to it and then slid out the window with the men's help.

There was a banging on the door to the barn just as Lizette slid over the window's edge.

"What did you have in your pickup?" Pete finally turned to Judd and asked. "I didn't figure you for a user."

"I'm not. I told him what the white stuff was. It's snow."

"Oh, man, he's going to be mad," Pete said with a grin on his face.

The gunshot echoed throughout the barn.

"Charley, the kids need a guard," Judd said as he and Pete overruled the older man's objection and lifted him out the window. "Get them all someplace safe."

Another gunshot echoed. This one sounded as if it struck metal, which meant Neal had hit the lock.

"Now you," Judd said to Pete.

But the cowboy was already building a barricade of metal chairs. "The others need a few minutes to get away from the window. There's no cover out this way."

Judd moved chairs, too. "I can be as distracting as any two men. No sense in both of us being in here."

Pete flashed him a grin. "I'm the Rat King. I don't run away."

Judd only grunted. He was a family man now. He didn't run away, either.

Something crashed against the barn door, and both Pete and Judd dived behind their shelter of metal chairs.

"Where are you?" Neal demanded as he swung the door wide open and stepped into the barn. "You think you can fool me. I'll show you."

It was silent for a moment. Then Neal said, "I see where you are. Think you can hide behind a pile of old chairs—now who's the fool?"

Judd grabbed one of the chairs. Neal would have to come close to them to actually have any hope of shooting them, and when he did, Judd intended to bash him over the head with one of these chairs. It wasn't much, but with God's help it might work.

Now, where did that thought come from? Judd wondered. It must be all this church he had been going to that gave him this nagging sense that he should be praying.

A loud creak sounded from the middle of the barn floor. Neal was walking this way.

Oh, well, Judd told himself, if he was going to die on his knees anyway, huddled behind a twisted mess of metal, he might as well figure out if God had any interest in him.

"Come out with your hands up!" The sound of the bullhorn made everyone jump.

Judd blinked. For a moment there, he'd thought that was God's voice answering his first feeble attempt at a prayer.

"What's going on?" Neal stood in the middle of the room and demanded.

"Come on out now with your hands up!" the voice on the bullhorn repeated. "We've got you surrounded."

"Ah, man," Neal said as he started walking toward the door. "All I was trying to do was get a good night's sleep."

Judd and Pete waited for the door to the barn to close before they stood up.

"Well," Pete said.

Judd nodded as he held out his hand to the other man.

Pete shook his hand. "Well."

Judd nodded.

Then they turned to walk out of the barn together.

Chapter Seventeen

Lizette wondered how she'd be able to hold the ballet without a Nutcracker. The Friday edition of the Billings newspaper had arrived on the counter in the hardware store, and the men hadn't stopped laughing since. On the first page was Edna Best's lead news story about the shoot-out in the Dry Creek barn. Gossip had circulated that story before the paper could, so the only real news was that the police officer who Neal had hit over the head was doing fine.

No, it was the sidebar to the story that was gathering everyone's interest this morning. The sidebar led to a human interest piece Edna had also written on the ballet that was tucked away on page twelve. The headline read, "Ballet Instructor Teaches Local Rancher, Judd Bowman, How to Kiss Like a Movie Star—Diagram Included."

Lizette's heart had stopped when she read the head-line. Her ballet performance was doomed. Judd would never show up.

Even more important, her friendship with him was doomed. He wouldn't want to be seen with her if people teased him about it, and no doubt some of those ranch hands at the hardware store were already thinking up clever things to say if they saw Judd and her together.

One thing Lizette knew about Judd was that he was a private person. He'd told her he hadn't talked to the people of Dry Creek for the first six months he'd lived here. She figured that was his way of warning her that he wasn't the cozy kind of person most women look for in a male friend. She had received the message and decided to ignore it. She didn't care if he was cozy or not. He was Judd.

She liked Judd and she wanted him to just be who he was. She'd wanted to get to know him better. She'd hoped maybe their friendship could grow into something more—maybe even the kind of love that people get married over.

But those hopes were all gone. Judd was probably home now planning how he could avoid the town of Dry Creek—and her—for the rest of his life.

It was hard to dream of a future with someone who never wanted to see you again.

Lizette couldn't exactly blame him, and she figured if he wasn't going to show up for the rest of her life, then he wasn't going to show up tonight either, so she'd best stop being sentimental and get on with the problem at hand. It was time, she told herself with a mental shake, to go with Plan B. Her heart hadn't been broken. Cracked maybe, but not broken. If she pulled herself together, she could think of a way to salvage the ballet performance tonight. That was what she wanted, wasn't it?

It was funny how the answer to that question was not as clear as it had once been.

In fact, after looking at the gun in Neal Strong's hand two days ago, Lizette had done a lot of thinking about what exactly her dreams were. She'd never been as scared for anyone else as she had been for those two children who were clinging to her legs.

Maybe it was time that ballet wasn't her only dream.

Madame Aprele had been staying in Mrs. Hargrove's spare room and helping with the last-minute preparations for the ballet performance. She could play the Nutcracker part if need be.

Lizette herself, she realized, had more important things to do right now.

There weren't many places in Dry Creek where a person could sit in silence and think. Lizette told herself that was why she headed for the church. It was as good a place as any, she reasoned, to take the things in her life and add them up so she'd know what she had.

Lizette wasn't halfway across the street before she heard the sound of a vehicle starting up behind the church. Somebody had already been there to see the pastor. Lizette wondered if a person was supposed to make an appointment. She'd have to ask.

Glory Curtis, the pastor's wife, was walking down the center aisle when Lizette stepped inside the church.

"Oh, hi," Glory said.

Lizette noticed the other woman didn't seem surprised to see her. "I don't have an appointment or anything."

Glory smiled. "You don't need an appointment. Most folks just know that my husband has office hours from nine to noon every day before he goes over to work the counter at the hardware store."

Lizette had heard the pastor partially supported himself by working in the hardware store. "I don't need to talk to him for long."

"Take your time."

The pastor himself didn't seem to be in any more of a hurry than his wife had been.

"I've never been to see a pastor before," Lizette confessed.

The pastor nodded. "Sometimes when people have

been through a traumatic event like having a gun pointed at them, they want to talk to someone. That's what I'm here for."

"I should be able to handle it myself. It's just that it sort of shook me up."

The pastor nodded. "Shook you up in what way?"

It seemed that the gun pointing at her had shaken her up in more ways than Lizette had thought. Her worries and concerns poured out of her. She'd even signed up for more meetings with the pastor. They were going to study the book of John together.

When Lizette left the church an hour later, she realized she'd completely forgotten about the ballet that was happening this evening. Even more amazing, she didn't start worrying when she did think about the ballet. She and the pastor had prayed, and God, she reasoned, would provide a Nutcracker.

The barn smelled like Christmas. Mrs. Hargrove and Charley had spent the afternoon bringing pine boughs down from the mountains and spreading them around the barn. The other scent was the warm smell of the sugar-plum pastries that Linda had baked this afternoon in the café ovens.

Lizette had gone back and forth between the café and the church doing last-minute things and being increasingly grateful for her friends. The Nutcracker performance might not live up to its ballet potential, but it was certainly living up to its friendship potential.

"Here, let me help you with that," Madame Aprele said as she walked alongside Lizette and offered to carry one of the trays Linda was lending them to display the pastries.

Lizette gave her the lightest of the trays. "If nothing else, people will like the pastries tonight."

Madame Aprele chuckled. "It'll all work out fine. You always used to make yourself sick worrying before any of your performances as a child. Remember, I used to say ballet is for fun."

Lizette grimaced. "It wasn't for fun in our house."

"I know," Madame Aprele said as they both stood on the cement area outside the barn. "I blame myself for not thinking of a way to bring your mother back into the ballet herself. Then she might not have demanded you do it for her."

"Oh, but she—" Lizette stopped herself. She'd never thought about the fact that her mother could still have danced. She might not have been able to do it professionally, but she could have danced in the productions at Madame Aprele's. She could have danced the ballet for fun.

Lizette opened the barn door and stood to one side so the other woman could enter.

"With your mother, it was all or nothing," Madame

Aprele said. "If she couldn't be the star of the show, she didn't want to be *in* the show."

Lizette nodded as they walked down to the end of the barn where the refreshment table was. "She used to say the same thing herself. Well, almost the same. She'd say if I wanted to dance, I should dance the main part."

Madame Aprele nodded as she put her tray on the table. "Ballet was never for the joy of it with your mother."

Lizette nodded as she set her tray down, as well. No, ballet was never for the pleasure of it with her mother. She wondered what her mother would do if one of her principal dancers didn't show for a ballet the way Lizette was expecting would happen tonight. Jacqueline would never forgive the dancer who didn't show, Lizette knew that much for sure.

For the first time in her life, Lizette didn't want to be like her mother.

Chapter Eighteen

The first group of people arrived in a noisy caravan of pickups from the Elkton ranch bunkhouse. It was snowing slightly, and the men stomped their feet on the cement outside the barn to knock any loose snow off their boots before they removed their hats and went inside the barn.

The Christmas tree in the stage area was lit with hundreds of tiny lights and all of the ornaments that Mrs. Hargrove generally hung on her tree. There were angels and red birds and golden sleighs. Someone, Lizette thought it had been Charley, had put a small wooden nativity set under the Christmas tree.

Lizette had all of the dancers, except for the Mouse King and the Nutcracker, up in the hayloft so that the audience wouldn't see their costumes until it was time for the ballet to begin. She had hung a blanket in a corner of the loft so they had a changing room, and all of the children were in their costumes. The children had peeked over the edge of the loft and whispered about how many people were in the audience. Even Mrs. Hargrove and Charley were standing near the edge of the loft.

They all saw Pete come in with his friends.

"We're up here," Lizette called, and Pete looked up to where she stood at the top of the stairs leading to the hayloft.

"I'm coming right up," Pete said as he left his friends.

"We still have a few more minutes," Madame Aprele said as she, too, walked to where the others stood and put her hand on Lizette's shoulder. "The children said Judd was coming. That he just had an errand to run in Miles City, and that he'd be back in time."

Lizette supposed she should be grateful that Judd had brought the children into town at least. "We'll have to go on without him if he's not here."

Mrs. Hargrove nodded. "There's still time for him to get here."

Lizette wondered if she could demand that everyone give her their copy of the diagram she'd drawn of how to stage a kiss. In all of the confusion, she'd left hers on the chair next to Edna. The reporter probably didn't even realize Lizette didn't want the diagram published.

It had just been an image to go with the text Edna had written. There were now thousands of that image between here and Billings. Some of them were going to be in the barn tonight.

Lizette looked over the rail of the loft and saw at least two ranch hands who had a piece of newsprint in their hands. It had to be the diagram.

There was probably no chance that Judd hadn't seen it, Lizette thought.

"Do you get a newspaper at your house?" Lizette turned and asked Bobby.

The boy shook his head. "Cousin Judd listens to the radio."

Maybe there *was* a chance, Lizette thought. Fortunately, no one on the radio was likely to have heard about the Hollywood Kiss Diagram, which was what Edna had referred to it as.

Fifteen more minutes passed and Judd still hadn't arrived. The barn had filled with a good-size crowd, and everyone seemed to be having a good time.

Lizette had decided she wouldn't sell tickets to the ballet, but Linda had offered to put a bucket near the refreshment table where people could make donations to cover the costs of the production. There was a line now for the coffee, and it looked like most people held a dollar bill in their hand to put in the bucket.

"I'll go down and get the music ready to start,"

Lizette said. It was five minutes until the time the ballet was scheduled to begin. She looked over at Madame Aprele and smiled. "You'd best get in the Nutcracker costume. When I come back up, I'll wait a few minutes and then give Linda the signal to dim the lights and push the play button for the music."

Lizette walked down the stairs and onto the barn floor. Half of the chairs were filled with people drinking coffee or punch and waiting for the ballet to begin. The other half of the chairs would comfortably seat the people who were still in line for their beverage.

Linda had suggested they serve the drinks before the ballet and then serve them again after the ballet when they brought out the pastries.

"Hi," Linda said when she saw Lizette walking toward the refreshment table. "We'll be finishing up here in a few minutes."

Lizette nodded. "Judd's not here yet, but he might not make it. When everyone gets settled down here and back to their seats, just dim the lights and then a minute later start the music. The dancers will come down the stairs then and we'll begin."

The chatter in the barn had a warm feeling to it, Lizette thought as she walked back to the stairs. People smiled and greeted her like an old friend instead of a performer, and she liked that.

Lizette climbed the stairs to the hayloft and gathered her dancers around her for a final word of encouragement.

"This is for fun," Lizette said to them all as she nodded to Madame Aprele, who was holding the Nutcracker's hat but still hadn't changed into the entire costume. The older woman had more hope than Lizette did. "I don't want you to worry if you make a mistake. Everything will be fine."

"I'm not going to make any mistakes," Amanda said. She had her costume on, and the wings glittered pink and gold in the light that came into the loft. "I'm a Sugar Plum Fairy, and we don't make mistakes."

"We try not to make mistakes," Lizette agreed. "But sometimes we do."

"Like Cousin Judd," Bobby said. "He's making a mistake because he's late."

Lizette put her hand on the boy's shoulder. "It's all right. It will be okay even if he doesn't get here. We'll all understand."

Lizette hoped that message would get to Judd through the children.

"Uh-uh." Amanda shook her head. "Cousin Judd needs to be here. He's the Nutcracker. Who's going to do the kiss if he's not here?"

Lizette exchanged a glance with Madame Aprele. The older woman would play the part of the Nutcracker. But— "Maybe there won't be a kiss this time around."

"I'd be happy to do the kiss," Pete said as he stepped out from behind the curtain in his Mouse King costume.

Lizette noticed the ranch hand had not flirted with her since he'd arrived. He wasn't even flirting now.

"On Judd's behalf, of course," Pete added. "As a friend."

"Oh, well—" Lizette stammered. "No one needs to do a kiss."

Pete stepped closer to the edge of the loft and looked over. "I think they're going to demand a kiss."

Lizette stepped closer to the edge of the loft just in time to see the barn door open.

"Well, look who's here," Pete said with relief. "I knew he'd make it."

It was Judd walking through the door, along with a woman who was wrapped in a long black coat with a gray wool scarf wrapped around her face so that none of her hair or skin showed.

Lizette tried not to be jealous of the fact that Judd was walking with his arm around the woman and leading her to one of the chairs in the back of the barn. Who Judd put his arm around was none of her business, Lizette told herself, even though he was carrying a huge bouquet of roses that he gave to the woman when she settled into her chair. Judd called Linda over to the woman before he looked up to the hayloft and saw Lizette and Pete.

The chatter in the barn grew more excited as Judd walked over to the staircase leading up to the hayloft.

"Cousin Judd!" Amanda squealed when she saw Judd coming up the stairs. "You came!"

"Of course," Judd said as he stood at the top of the stairs.

"You need to get into your costume," Pete said as he slapped Judd on the back. "We've got a ballet to do."

Linda dimmed the lights to signal the audience was ready. Judd was already walking over to Madame Aprele, who held out his costume to him. Then he headed for the curtain to change. "If you want to start, I can slip down in a few minutes."

Lizette nodded. "You don't need to be in the first few minutes, anyway. We thought we'd have the family sing a carol in front of the tree to start."

This, Lizette thought, was what a family Christmas felt like even hundreds of years ago when the Nutcracker was written. It was gathering your friends and family together beside a tree and celebrating a wonderful time of gifts and love.

The carol the family sang was "Silent Night." Mrs. Hargrove led everyone in the barn in softly singing the song and the sound filled the whole structure with warmth.

Lizette slowly danced ballet steps to show how a young girl would see the wonder of that night long ago when Christ was born. The audience was hushed.

Lizette had not known until these past few days what it meant to be truly silent on that holy night.

After the carol finished, Charley started to read the story of the Nutcracker.

The Nutcracker came on the stage just when the presents were given to the children, and Lizette realized what she should have done. She should have taken a moment to warn Judd about the kiss. He must not know that everyone had been talking about the kiss he was going to give her tonight.

Lizette danced the part of Clara's excitement over her new gift, hoping to come close enough to whisper in Judd's ear. Unfortunately, none of the steps got her close enough to say a few words to him that all of the others wouldn't also hear.

She'd have to wait for the battle scene, she thought. There would be enough noise with all of the mice attacking that no one would hear her talking to Judd.

What was wrong with the Nutcracker? When they had practiced, Judd had held back as though he wasn't part of the mice attack. He'd let the children attack him, but he hadn't gotten into their play. Now, he attacked with abandon, lifting one mouse up in the air until the mouse giggled and then going after another until even the tin soldier forgot which side of the battle he was on and all of the children swarmed around the Nutcracker.

Lizette didn't have a chance to talk to Judd, so she

just kept dancing. She twisted and turned and made it look like the whole stage was alive with ballet.

Then Charley started to read about the attack of the Mouse King, and Pete burst out of the fireplace with a roar that briefly overpowered the music.

Now, Lizette said to herself, as she tried to dance closer to Judd to explain that he didn't need to kiss her. There wasn't a kiss in every Nutcracker production, and there wouldn't be one in this one. The people of Dry Creek would have to get their romance elsewhere this Christmas. Her friendship with Judd was more important than the ballet, even if this ballet affected the future of her ballet school in this little community where she was making her home.

"Psst," Lizette hissed as she danced as close as she could to Pete and Judd.

The Mouse King and the Nutcracker were engaged in a magnificent battle, and the audience was shouting encouragement to them both. There was enough noise that she could deliver her message to Judd if he'd only look her way.

But the Mouse King had the Nutcracker in his grip, and Charley was clearing his throat.

"The shoe." Judd twisted his neck and finally looked at Lizette. "You need to throw your shoe."

Lizette figured she'd have to talk to Judd after she saved his life.

Lizette's shoe hit Pete on the shoulder, and he went down with a groan.

The music swelled up and Charley threw sparkling confetti in the air as if it was a party.

Judd moved closer.

Finally, Lizette thought as she danced closer to him, she'd have a chance to tell him about the kiss.

"You don't need to do the kiss," Lizette whispered as she came close to Judd.

Judd had already taken his hat off, and he wasn't frowning at all. In fact, Lizette thought he looked downright happy. Which meant only one thing. He hadn't heard about the story in the newspaper.

"Oh, yes, I do," Judd said as he moved even closer to her until she had no room left to dance.

"But—" Lizette said before Judd bent down and kissed her. It wasn't a stage kiss, of course. He hadn't taken any of her earlier suggestions. The funny thing was that she didn't care. She had his kiss.

Yes, she thought to herself, this was what Christmas and mistletoe and family were all about.

Lizette was only dimly aware of the applause.

"We're not finished," she murmured as she settled even closer to Judd, if that was possible.

"Not by a long shot," Judd agreed with his lips close to hers.

"We still have the Sugar Plum Fairy."

"That, too," Judd agreed as he smiled into her eyes and then kissed her again.

The applause overpowered the music. Lizette thought there was some stomping, too.

"Oh, yes," Judd said as he slowly pulled himself away from her. "I almost forgot—"

Judd looked to his side where Linda stood with the hugest bouquet of red roses Lizette had ever seen.

"These are for you," Judd said to her as he took the roses from Linda and handed them to Lizette.

She almost cried. Everything was perfect for the moment. But when someone said something about that diagram, she didn't know what he would do.

Judd then turned to the audience and said quite clearly, "And for those of you who are wondering about the secret to a Hollywood kiss, that's it. Bring her roses, boys, that's all there is to it."

The audience loved him. Lizette could see that. Odd that she still had the urge to cry.

"That was a smart move," she said to Judd. She couldn't look him in the eye, but she could look at his chin, which was close enough. "They won't tease you now. It was brilliant."

"Brilliant had nothing to do with it," Judd whispered as he tipped her chin up so her eyes met his. "I'm hoping to kiss you a lot in the days ahead, and I don't want someone stopping to draw a diagram of it every time I do."

"You do? Hope to kiss me?"

Judd nodded. "A man's got to have hope even if he's got no reason to."

Lizette smiled. "You have reason."

Judd grinned and kissed her again.

Lizette danced the next scenes as she had never danced before. Madame Aprele was right about ballet being fun. The Snow Queen must have thought it was fun, too, because she almost frolicked during her scenes.

Then there was the Sugar Plum Fairy. Amanda glowed as she stood at the edge of the stage area and started her dance. Lizette had had more time to teach Amanda dance steps than any of her other students, and the little girl was actually doing ballet.

Lizette had given Amanda a solo part, and so Lizette had danced to the sidelines to wait while Amanda completed it.

Madame Aprele was standing next to Lizette. "She's got promise, that one. She's a natural."

Lizette nodded. It was good to know she had at least one student who was in it for the ballet instead of the doughnuts.

"There will be more," Madame Aprele said with a nod to the audience. "You'll find more students out there."

The applause at the end of Amanda's solo was as

loud as the kiss applause, and the little girl glowed under the shower of encouragement until one woman at the back of the seating area stood up to give her a standing ovation.

"Mama," Amanda squealed, and forgot all about being the Sugar Plum Fairy as she ran down the aisle to her mother.

Lizette swore there wasn't a dry eye in the whole barn by the end of the ballet.

Chapter Nineteen

"We're going to need more napkins," Linda announced as Lizette managed to walk through the crowd of well-wishers in order to check with Linda on how things were going. "Next time we should forget asking for contributions for coffee and just sell handkerchiefs. We'll make a fortune. Even I was teary-eyed."

"Who wouldn't cry when Amanda saw her mother?"

"And you and Judd," Linda said as she reached for a napkin. "That sent me over the edge."

"Well—" Lizette wanted to admit that it had sent *her* over the edge, too, but the man was nowhere around and so she wasn't sure she should be thinking what she was thinking, so she didn't want to say anything.

"I mean, when he gave you the second kiss, I knew— that's the real thing." Linda dabbed at her eyes. "Judd's just so romantic. My boyfriend used to be that way, too."

Lizette couldn't help but think it would be a lot more romantic if Judd had actually hung around to talk to her after a kiss like that. At first she thought he was with the kids and their mother, but she'd looked over there and he wasn't with them, either. She'd heard that Judd's cousin had been in a hospital in Colorado until Sheriff Wall went there to convince her it was safe to come back. Judd had met her in Miles City and brought her out to the performance. After such a long day, maybe Judd was just tired. Maybe he'd just gone home without a word to anyone.

"Ah, there he is," Linda said.

Lizette turned to look in the direction of Linda's gaze.

So there was Judd, coming in the door with Pete right behind him. They were both still in costume although they had put on their hats and their coats, so they looked a little odd.

Lizette could see Judd scanning the crowd and looking for someone until his eyes found hers and the scanning stopped. He started walking toward her.

"If you'll excuse me," Linda said as she started to walk away from Lizette. "I think three might be a crowd right about now."

"Sorry," Judd said as he stopped in front of Lizette. "I had to give Pete a key to my place and I'd left the key in my pickup."

"Pete?"

"Yeah, I told him he could stay at my place for a few days until the teasing dies down about his tail."

Lizette smiled. "I didn't think of that."

"Yeah, this having-a-friend business is a commitment, you know," Judd said as he reached out and touched Lizette on the cheek. "Not that I'm opposed to commitments anymore. I want you to know that. In fact, there's one commitment I'll welcome if I get a chance to make it."

"What's that?" Lizette said.

"This one." Judd bent his head to kiss her.

Epilogue

From the Dry Creek Tidbits column appearing in the March 17 issue of the Billings newspaper:

The bride, Lizette Baker, and the groom, Judd Bowman, were married in the church in Dry Creek last Saturday, March 14, at two o'clock in the afternoon. The groom's little cousin, Amanda Strong, was the flower girl and her brother, Bobby Strong, was the ring bearer.

Both children (who take lessons at the Baker School of Ballet along with eight other children) executed perfect pirouettes on their way down the aisle as a special gift to their ballet teacher.

The bride and groom gave special thanks to the pastor of the church, who had baptized them and received their confession of faith several months prior to their marriage.

Doughnuts were served at the reception along with a five-tiered wedding cake, both made by the bride, who offers her baking services at the Dry Creek Café.

Readers of this column who want to send congratulation cards to Mr. and Mrs. Bowman can send cards to the Bowman Ranch, Dry Creek, Montana (the groom assured me there is no need to refer to their place as the Jenkins place any longer and I believe he's right. It's now the Bowman family's place.)

Readers of this column will also remember that the bride and groom were engaged shortly after demonstrating the Hollywood kiss that was diagrammed in this column. Their kiss after the wedding ceremony rivaled the one many readers saw at the Nutcracker ballet performance before Christmas.

The bride was quoted as saying, "Finally, we have that kiss just right."

The groom offered to keep practicing.

* * * * *

Dear Reader,

I hope you enjoyed reading about Judd and Lizette. When I was telling their story, I thought about what it feels like to go to a church for the first time. Their feelings of awkwardness are repeated many times each Sunday as someone visits a church and isn't sure of what their welcome will be. During the Christmas season, you may see people in your church who do not seem to feel comfortable. Hopefully, you can help them feel like they are among friends.

May you have a blessed Christmas.

Janet Tronstad

If you liked the FAITH ON THE LINE *series
from Love Inspired, you'll love the*
FAITH AT THE CROSSROADS *series,
coming in January
from Love Inspired Suspense!*

*And now, turn the page for
a sneak preview of* A TIME TO PROTECT
by Lois Richer, the first installment of
FAITH AT THE CROSSROADS.

*On sale in January 2006
from Steeple Hill Books.*

Brendan Montgomery switched his beeper to vibrate and slid it back inside his shirt pocket. Nothing was going to spoil Manuel DeSantis Vance's first birthday party—and this large Vance and Montgomery gathering—if he could help it.

Peter Vance's puffed-out chest needed little explanation. He was as formidable as any father proudly displaying his beloved child. Peter's wife Emily waited on Manuel's other side, posing for the numerous photographs Yvette Duncan insisted posterity demanded. Apparently posterity was greedy.

Judging by the angle of her camera, Brendan had a hunch Yvette's lens sidetracked from the parents to the cake she'd made for Manuel. Who could blame her? That intricate train affair must have taken hours to create and assemble, and little Manuel obviously appreciated her efforts.

"Make sure you don't chop off their heads this time,

Yvette." As the former mayor of Colorado Springs, Frank Montgomery had opinions on everything. And as Yvette's mentor, he'd never been shy about offering her his opinion, especially on all aspects of picture-taking. But since Yvette's camera happened to be the latest in digital technology and Frank had never owned one, Brendan figured most of his uncle's free advice was superfluous and probably useless. But he wouldn't be the one to tell him so.

"Don't tell me what to do, Frank," Yvette ordered, adjusting the camera. "Just put your arm around your wife. Liza, can you get him to smile?" Satisfied, Yvette motioned for Dr. Robert Fletcher and his wife Pamela, who were Manuel's godparents, and their two young sons, to line up behind the birthday boy.

Brendan eased his way into the living room and found a horde of Montgomery and Vance family members lounging around the room, listening to a news report on the big-screen television.

"Alistair Barclay, the British hotel mogul now infamous for his ties to a Latin American drug cartel, died today under suspicious circumstances. Currently in jail, Barclay was accused of running a branch of the notorious crime syndicate right here in Colorado Springs. The drug cartel originated in Venezuela under the direction of kingpin Baltasar Escalante, whose private plane crashed some months ago while he was attempting to escape the CIA. Residents of Colorado Springs have worked long and hard to free their city from the grip of crime—"

"Hey, guys, this is a party. Let's lighten up." Brendan reached out and pressed the mute button, followed by a chorus of groans. "You can listen to the same newscast tonight, but we don't want to spoil Manuel's big day with talk of drug cartels and death, do we?"

His brother Quinn winked and took up his cause. "Yeah, what's happening with that cake, anyway? Are we ever going to eat it? I'm starving."

"So is somebody else, apparently," Yvette said, appearing in the doorway, her flushed face wreathed in a grin. "Manuel already got his thumb onto the train track and now he's covered in black icing. His momma told him he had to wait 'til the mayor gets here, though, so I guess you'll just have to do the same, Quinn."

Good-natured groans filled the room.

"Maxwell Vance has been late since he got elected into office," Fiona Montgomery said, her eyes dancing with fun. "Maybe one of us should give him a call and remind him his grandson is waiting for his birthday cake. In fact, I'll do it myself."

"Leave the mayor alone, Mother. He already knows your opinion on pretty much everything," Brendan said, sharing a grin with Quinn.

"It may be that the mayor has been delayed by some

important meeting," Alessandro Donato spoke up from his seat in the corner. "After Thanksgiving, that is the time when city councilors and mayors iron out their budgets, yes?"

"But just yesterday I talked to our mayor about that, in regard to a story I'm doing on city finances." Brendan's cousin Colleen sat cross-legged on the floor, her hair tied back into the eternal ponytail she favored. "He said they hadn't started yet."

Something about the way Alessandro moved when he heard Colleen's comment sent a nerve in Brendan's neck to twitching, enough to make him take a second look at the man. Moving up through the ranks of the FBI after his time as a police officer had only happened because Brendan usually paid attention to that nerve. Right now it was telling him to keep an eye on the tall, lean man named Alessandro, even if he was Lidia Vance's nephew.

There was something about Alessandro that didn't quite fit. What was the story on this guy anyway?

A phone rang. Brendan chuckled when everyone in the room checked their pockets. His grin faded when Alessandro spoke into his. His face paled, his body tensed. He murmured one word then listened.

"Hey, something's happening! Turn up the TV, Brendan," Colleen said. Everyone was staring at the screen where a reporter stood in front of City Hall.

Brendan raised the volume.

"Mayor Vance was apparently on his way to a family event when the shot was fired. Excuse me, I'm getting an update." The reporter lifted one hand to press the earpiece closer. "I'm told there may have been more than one shot fired. As I said, at this moment, Maxwell Vance is on his way to the hospital. Witnesses say he was bleeding profusely from his head and chest, though we have no confirmed details. We'll update you as the situation develops."

LARGER PRINT BOOKS!

2 FREE LARGER PRINT NOVELS PLUS A FREE MYSTERY GIFT

Love Inspired®

Larger print novels are now available...

YES! Please send me 2 FREE LARGER PRINT Love Inspired® novels and my FREE mystery gift. After receiving them, if I don't wish to receive any more books, I can return the shipping statement marked "cancel." If I don't cancel, I will receive 4 brand-new novels every month and be billed just $4.24 per book in the U.S., or $4.99 per book in Canada, plus 25¢ shipping and handling per book and applicable taxes, if any*. That's a savings of over 20% off the cover price! I understand that accepting the 2 free books and gift places me under no obligation to buy anything. I can always return a shipment and cancel at any time. Even if I never buy another book from Steeple Hill, the two free books and gift are mine to keep forever.

121 IDN D733   321 IDN D74F

Name	(PLEASE PRINT)	
Address		Apt.
City	State/Prov.	Zip/Postal Code

Signature (if under 18, a parent or guardian must sign)

Order online at www.LoveInspiredBooks.com

Or mail to Steeple Hill Reader Service™:

IN U.S.A.	IN CANADA
3010 Walden Ave.	P.O. Box 609
P.O. Box 1867	Fort Erie, Ontario
Buffalo, NY 14240-1867	L2A 5X3

Are you a current Love Inspired subscriber and want to receive the larger print edition?

Call 1-800-221-5011 today!

* Terms and prices subject to change without notice. NY residents add applicable sales tax. Canadian residents will be charged applicable provincial taxes and GST. This offer is limited to one order per household. All orders subject to approval. Credit or debit balances in a customer's account(s) may be offset by any other outstanding balance owed by or to the customer.

LILPO05

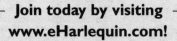

Love Inspired®

TITLES AVAILABLE NEXT MONTH

Don't miss these four stories in January

A FAMILY TO SHARE by Arlene James
Connie Wheeler's relationship choices landed her in jail.
Yet the single mother's new job caring for Kendal Oakes's
troubled daughter helped her blossom, even as it brought
her closer to the little girl's father. But would he stand by
her when her past was revealed?

HOME TO YOU by Cheryl Wolverton
Faced with a devastating diagnosis, Meghan O'Halleran had
no one to turn to. Though she hadn't seen him in twenty years,
childhood friend Dakota "Cody" Ryder was her only hope.
The memory of that friendship shone like a beacon, guiding
her home once more. Would welcoming arms await her?

MATCHMAKER, MATCHMAKER… by Anna Schmidt
A fluff piece on Grace Harrison's Christian speed-dating program
was all well and good for reporter Jud Marlowe, but his instincts
told him a different story lay with her senator father. If only Grace
weren't so…*appealing*. With the article in question, it was up to
Jud to decide what was more important—a scoop or a sweetheart.

HIS BUNDLE OF LOVE by Patricia Davids
When the pregnant woman he'd taken to the hospital named
him as her child's father before slipping into a coma, EMT
Mick O'Callaghan was floored. He couldn't have children of
his own, and baby Beth melted his heart. And as the new mother
recovered, he couldn't help wanting to take care of her, too….

LICNM1205